GOLD COAST ANGELS

**The hottest docs, the warmest hearts,
the highest drama**

Gold Coast City Hospital is located
right in Australia's Surfers Paradise, at the
heart of the Gold Coast, just a stone's throw
away from the world famous beach.
The hospital has a reputation for some of
the finest doctors in their field, kind-hearted
nurses and cutting-edge treatments.

With their 'work hard and play hard' motto,
the staff form a warm, vibrant community
where rumours, passion and drama are
never far away. Especially when
there is a new arrival—
fresh from Angel Mendez Hospital, NYC!

**When utterly gorgeous
bad-boy-with-a-heart Cade
rolls into town, trouble is definitely
coming to Surfers Paradise!**

If you loved **NYC Angels**,
you'll love the high drama and passion
of this irresistible four-book
Mills & Boon® Medical Romance™ series!

**GOLD COAST ANGELS:
HOW TO RESIST TEMPTATION**
by Amy Andrews

is also available this month

Dear Reader

Almost everyone in Australia would associate the Gold Coast, Queensland, with theme parks, beaches, holidays and fun. Everyone except, of course, the people who live there. For them it's just home. They get to enjoy the lovely beaches and the tranquillity of the rainforest in their own back gardens. Last year, when I was at a conference of romance writers on the Gold Coast, I wondered what it would be like to live in a tourist town—because everyday life isn't vacation...it's everyday life! How often do the residents get to the beach or the rainforest?

So, when my editor asked me if I would like to be part of the *Gold Coast Angels* series I leaped at the chance, because this was my opportunity to explore living and working in a place that ticked 24/7 with a holiday vibe but was still home to so many people.

Chloe hasn't really ever had a vacation, even though she's lived on the Gold Coast for a decade. She's been too busy supporting her brother Nick and getting her own life back together after being abandoned by her parents at sixteen. Now she's just turned thirty, and she's reflecting on her life and where it's headed. Have the sacrifices she's been forced to make been worth it?

Luke loved the casual Gold Coast lifestyle in the huge house on the canal that he shared with his wife and daughter, but one moment in time stole all that from him. Now he's living in a town known for its fun, and yet he's cloaked in sadness and not able to see a way out of it.

I hope you enjoy Chloe and Luke's story, set against the backdrop of sun, surf and life lived to the full, and seeing how they manage against the odds to find their place in it and each other.

For photos of the Gold Coast, and tourist information to help you plan your next vacation, head over to my website: www.fionalowe.com. I love to hear from my readers, and you can find me on Facebook, Twitter, Goodreads, my website and blog, or e-mail me at fiona@fionalowe.com

Happy Reading!

Fiona x

'I knew when I picked up a Fiona Lowe title
that I was going to be reading a spellbinding story
which I would devour in one sitting.'
—*Contemporary Romance Reviews* on
SYDNEY HARBOUR HOSPITAL: TOM'S REDEMPTION

GOLD COAST ANGELS: BUNDLE OF TROUBLE

BY
FIONA LOWE

First published in Great Britain 2013
by Mills & Boon, an imprint of Harlequin (UK) Limited,
Large Print edition 2014
Eton House, 18-24 Paradise Road,
Richmond, Surrey, TW9 1SR

© 2013 Harlequin Books S.A.

Special thanks and acknowledgment are
given to Fiona Lowe for her contribution to the
Gold Coast Angels series
ISBN: 978 0 263 23872 3

Always an avid reader, **Fiona Lowe** decided to combine her love of romance with her interest in all things medical, so writing Mills & Boon® Medical Romance™ was an obvious choice! She lives in a seaside town in southern Australia, where she juggles writing, reading, working and raising two gorgeous sons with the support of her own real-life hero!

Recent books by the same author:

NEWBORN BABY FOR CHRISTMAS
LETTING GO WITH DR RODRIGUEZ
SYDNEY HARBOUR HOSPITAL:
  TOM'S REDEMPTION
CAREER GIRL IN THE COUNTRY
SINGLE DAD'S TRIPLE TROUBLE
THE MOST MAGICAL GIFT OF ALL
HER BROODING ITALIAN SURGEON
MIRACLE: TWIN BABIES

These books are also available in eBook format from www.millsandboon.co.uk

To Kath for sharing her story
and to Christine for telling it.
Wishing you both good health and happiness.

CHAPTER ONE

'HAPPY BIRTHDAY!'

The cheers rained over Chloe Kefes and she didn't know if she wanted to laugh, cry or run. Truth be told, she wanted to do all three as she stared in shocked surprise at the smiling faces of her colleagues.

Somehow she managed to get her legs to move and as she stepped forward into the meeting room, the staff enthusiastically rushed her with balloons and hugs before pressing a polystyrene cup containing a small drop of champagne into her hand. So much for this being a vital patient review meeting on the busy Gold Coast City Hospital's plastic surgery ward—instead it was a well-meant ambush.

'To Chloe.' They raised their cups.

'Many happy returns, Clo.'

'Have a good one.'

Her shoulders were squeezed, she was patted on the back, and her arm was pummelled with birthday bumps as half the room—the afternoon shift—rushed past her, dashing back to work.

'Don't let Richard eat all the Tim Tams,' Julie, the radiographer, called out over her shoulder.

Their departure left behind the now off-duty day staff, which comprised a student nurse, a medical student and the plastics registrar, Richard, who had a reputation for eating all the chocolates.

Chloe finally found her voice. 'Oh, you guys, you didn't have to do this.' *Really, I wish you hadn't.*

Keri Letterman, the unit nurse manager, gave her a wide smile. 'You didn't think we'd let the big *three-oh* go past without acknowledging it, now, did you?'

'Wow,' muttered the barely twenty-year-old student nurse to the twenty-one-year-old med student, 'I didn't think she was that old.'

Chloe tried to give the bright and breezy smile she was known for but, despite her very best attempt, her 'I guess not' came out a tad strangled.

Up until a few minutes ago she'd really thought she'd managed to slip under the birthday police's radar, otherwise known as Keri and Kate. Given the fuss they'd made of Lizzie, the ward clerk, on her fiftieth birthday, Chloe probably should have known better. Except that, unlike the rest of the staff, she hadn't spent the preceding days giving a birthday countdown to anyone who'd listen.

In fact, she hadn't told anyone it was her birthday and she certainly hadn't told them it was the dreaded thirtieth.

'Lucky for you,' Keri continued, 'I met Nick, Lucy and those gorgeous twins in the cafeteria and they told me it was your special day. If we were depending on you to tell us, we'd never have known.'

That was the general idea. 'Who needs enemies when you've got a big brother, right?' Chloe joked, hearing the slight criticism in her boss's voice. She worked on letting it slide over her. Unlike many of her colleagues, she didn't bring her private life to work—mostly because she didn't have one.

Instead, she chatted about her new apartment

with the sea view—a ten-centimetre glimpse of the ocean from her kitchen sink—her bushwalks in the rainforest hinterland around Mt Warning, and her latest adventures with sea kayaking. All of it kept the conversation firmly off the very personal.

Her reticence to share stemmed from experience. She'd learned a long time ago that the more you told people about your life, the more questions they asked, and she was only prepared to talk about the last couple of years. Any further back didn't bear thinking about.

'So what did you get for your birthday, Chloe?' Richard asked, licking chocolate off his fingers.

She slid a photo out of her pocket and metaphorically crossed her fingers that the sheer cuteness factor of the photo would forestall the inevitable comments. 'Chester.'

'Oh, my God! He's just like the puppy on the toilet-paper ads,' Kate, a fellow nurse, gushed. 'How old is he?'

'Eight weeks.'

'That's little.' Kate frowned. 'Who's looking after him while you're at work?'

'He's at doggie daycare.'

'Doggie daycare?' Richard rolled his eyes. 'Showing us photos of a dog is a sure sign you need a man and a baby.'

Chloe tried unsuccessfully not to let his words slap her. Richard was a congenial guy who had no idea his off-the-cuff comment encapsulated everything she wanted in her life but could never have. 'Dogs are so much easier,' she tried to quip lightly, 'and, unlike you, my puppy will eventually be house-trained.'

Richard laughed good-naturedly as his pager beeped. Grabbing the last two Tim Tams before Kate could stop him, he called the students to follow him and he left with a wicked grin.

Keri looked at the photo of Chester. 'He *is* cute. Did I show you the photo of Tahlia dressed up as a cat?'

'You did.' Chloe tried to stop the smile on her face from freezing. She'd seen every photo of Tahlia from a wet, slippery newborn on her mother's chest right up to the most recent ones taken on her second birthday. Keri, like most proud parents, loved to spread her mother joy around, sharing every milestone with anyone and everyone who would listen. If they didn't want to listen, she told them anyway.

'Jack's off his training wheels.' Kate pulled out her phone and brought up a photo of her second son.

'He looks so grown up,' Keri said.

'I know, right? I remember the day he took his first step and now he's six and riding his own bike.' Kate scrolled to another photo. 'Chloe, you have to see this one.'

'Lovely,' Chloe said faintly. Chester's photo was supposed to be her weapon against this sort of thing but instead the cuteness of the puppy seemed to be reminding everyone else that their children were cute too.

'You okay, Chloe?' Keri asked

She renewed her smile, putting extra wattage into it. 'Fine, why?'

'You're shredding the rim of your cup.'

'I must need more champagne, then.' She picked up the bottle and sloshed in more of the straw-coloured liquid before gulping it down.

Kate held out her cup for a refill. 'What are your plans for tonight?'

A walk along the beach with Chester, followed by take-out Indian and then tucking up in bed and watching all four hours of North and South. Only Kate, who was married with young kids and had rose-coloured memories of being single, would be horrified at the thought. 'I'm hitting *The Bedroom* with some friends.' It wasn't strictly a lie.

Kate's eyes lit up. 'Oh, I remember nightclubs. Good for you, Chloe.'

'I bet Nick and Lucy have plans to spoil you,' Keri said as she started to tidy up the remains of the food.

She thought of her wonderful and loving brother, who'd been her sole supporter since she was sixteen. They'd been through a huge amount together and their joint determination to succeed had kept the other going during the tougher times.

Nick's recent marriage was wonderful and she'd been thrilled he'd found such a supportive life partner in Lucy but, as expected, the wedding and the arrival of the twins had changed things between them. His focus was now on his wife and children, not his sister, which was right and proper—and as much as she loved the twins she found it excruciatingly hard to be around them. All of it meant there were times she missed Nick very much.

'Nick organised for Café Sunset to open at six and we ate breakfast watching the sunrise—'

'Sorry to interrupt the party.'

Chloe swung around at the deep and slightly disdainful voice that didn't sound sorry at all.

'Luke?' Keri squealed with delight, and rushed forward, hugging him hard.

His body stiffened and he closed his eyes for a moment, as if he was seeking a way to endure the affection.

Chloe blinked and then gave her glasses a surreptitious polish and took another look. Was this gaunt man with a spray of silver at his temples really Luke Stanley? The eminent plastic surgeon who was known for his good humour and easygoing manner? She scanned her memory, barely recognising him.

She didn't know him personally—in fact she'd

only ever had one brief encounter with him and that had been well over a year ago. Just thinking about it made her cheeks burn with embarrassment. It had been her first day on the ward.

Due to her age, everyone had assumed she'd been nursing for years, but her education had been truncated at sixteen and it had taken her a few years to return to study. Graduating from university at twenty-eight had meant she'd had to work doubly hard to appear totally competent compared with the younger nurses for whom other staff members automatically made allowances on account of their youth and inexperience.

With that in mind, back on her first day she'd been busy concentrating on preparing a dressing pack by a patient's bed, readying to check the skin edges, where his finger had been stitched back in place. As she had been mentally checking off all the items she required, she'd suddenly heard a deep and booming voice behind her saying, 'Hello, Mr Benjamin.'

Startled, she'd swung around fast, completely forgetting she'd been holding an open container of iodine. The sudden movement had propelled the brown liquid out of the bottle, sending it flying up into the air where it had paused for a perilous moment—mocking her and her total lack of control over its trajectory. Gravity had pulled it down fast and it had landed on Mr Stanley, plastic surgeon, and, to all intents and purposes, her new boss.

As the indelible dark stain had oozed down his striped shirt, his crystal-clear green eyes had widened in surprise.

'Oh, God, I'm s-so s-sorry,' she stammered. 'Of course I'll replace it.' Juggling this month's bills to pay for what was probably a two-hundred-dollar shirt would involve robbing Peter to pay Paul—otherwise known as raiding her car fund yet again.

He raised his head—his neatly clipped and styled jet-black curls barely moving—and he smiled. 'This is the third hit this shirt's taken today. My wife frowns whenever I wear it as apparently it's not my colour and I shouldn't be trusted to shop alone,' he said with good humour. 'My baby daughter added her opinion by sicking up on it this morning just as I was racing out the door, and now this. I think you may have done me a favour… I'm sorry, I don't know your name.'

'Kefes. Chloe Kefes. I'm new today.'

Mr Benjamin, bless him, chimed in with, 'She's been taking excellent care of me, Doc.'

'I'm sure she has.' Luke tilted his head in contemplation. 'Our obstetrician's surname was Kefes. He works here at Gold Coast City and I think my wife secretly fell in love with him when he delivered Amber.' He laughed and pulled out his phone, showing her a photo of a newborn baby in a bath.

With huge, dark eyes and a thatch of black hair, the baby, like all newborns, looked unmistakably like her father. Chloe thought of a baby lost in the mists of time and she teetered on the edge of darkness.

'This is Amber an hour after Nick delivered her,' he said fondly. 'Believe me, I was in awe of him as well. I don't suppose he's any relation?'

She grabbed onto the lifeline of a conversation about her brother—one far removed from babies—and said, 'Actually, Nick's my brother and he is pretty awe-inspiring.'

Nick had sacrificed a lot and worked really hard to get to where he was today and she loved hearing how well regarded he was in the community.

Luke's smile widened. 'Caring professions must run in your family. Did you grow up in a medical household?'

She shook her head, not wanting to go anywhere near that mess of tangled and fraught emotions. 'Are you sure you're okay about your shirt?'

Again his ready smile graced his tanned cheeks. 'Please don't worry about it. Chances are Anna will probably write you a thank-you note for making it unwearable.' He turned his attention to his patient. 'So, Mr Benjamin, I just want to have a look at your fingers and see if my handiwork has counteracted the impact of the circular saw.'

That was the last time she'd seen him until today. Soon after the iodine debacle, a memo had been sent out from medical administration stating that Luke Stanley was on sabbatical for a year. At the time she hadn't thought anything of it. Consultants came and went, and her job was all about the patients. But now, looking at him, she wondered if he'd been on sabbatical in a place that lacked sunshine. The man who once could have been glibly described as tall, dark, tanned, charming and with a ready smile looked pale, tired and tense.

Keri smiled as she stepped back from the hug. 'I saw your name was back on the surgery list and I was wondering when you'd come up and say hi.' She extended her arm. 'You remember Kate, but I don't think you've met Chloe.'

Kate raised her hand in greeting. 'Welcome back, Luke.'

'Thanks.' The gruff word lacked grace.

Then eyes that Chloe remembered as having been bright and full of fun swung a dull gaze at her. No sign of recognition registered in their mossy dark depths. He gave her a curt nod of acknowledgment and an unruly curl fell across a slanted black eyebrow, highlighting his general dishevelment.

The inky stubble on his jaw had passed the three-day requirement of fashionable growth and now cried out for the tidying touch of a razor. Instead of a crisp shirt tucked into a pair of tailored suit trousers, he wore a dark red polo shirt and crumpled chinos that looked as if he'd slept in them. Perhaps he was jet-lagged and had just got off the plane?

He swung his attention back to Keri. 'I've got a complicated surgery this week on a child the foundation's brought over from Bali. He's got shocking scarring on his neck and face due to the burn of hot oil and he can't close his mouth or move his head. He'll need one-on-one nursing and I want him nursed here by a plastics nurse, not in Paediatrics.'

Keri nodded. 'What day are we talking?'

'Thursday.'

The unit manager consulted the nursing roster on the notice-board. 'Chloe's rostered on through Sunday.'

'Good,' Luke said, sounding weary and resigned, as if everything was an effort but at least one job had been sorted out.

No, not good at all. A mild flutter of anxiety batted Chloe's chest. She nursed adults and she didn't like where this conversation was heading at all.

Luke's gaze raked her again—a desolate look in his eyes calling up a sadness in her that she knew only too well. A sadness she'd learned to avoid thinking about. As she tried to shake off the melancholy his glance had elicited, she caught a momentary flash of something in his eyes that lit up the brilliant green.

A tingle shot up her spine, leaving a trail of unsettling effervescence. A tingle she barely re-membered and had only *ever* associated with pain and regret. A tingle that had absolutely no place in this situation. He was married with a child and she wasn't the sort of woman who would ever break up a marriage. Never. Ever.

She tried to throw off the sensation. Ethics aside, she didn't even know him, so why a flut-ter of attraction? Her body, unlike her brain, must have its wires utterly crossed. Empathy was the *only* thing she should be feeling for this man— empathy generated by the sadness in his eyes— nothing else. Definitely not lust.

'...at eight in the operating theatre, Chloe.'

The way his tongue rolled over her name shocked her back into the conversation and with her heart thumping hard she threw a beseeching look at Keri. 'Jackie has way more experience than I do working with children.'

'She does,' Keri agreed, 'but she's not rostered on and you are.'

Chloe thought of her empty social calendar. 'I can swap.'

Keri shook her head. 'She's got her sister's wedding, remember?'

She turned to Kate, trying to hold her desperation in check. 'How about you, Kate? As a birthday gift to me?'

'Sorry, Chloe, I've got a family thing on. You know how it is.'

She didn't know at all. Apart from meals with Nick, she hadn't had a *family thing* in fourteen years.

A sigh of frustration hissed from Luke's thinned lips and it bounced around the room, loud in its disapproval. He zeroed his glare onto her. The ominous, dark look made his high cheekbones sharp and stark, which emphasised the charcoal shadows under his eyes. 'I'm sorry if my plans are inconveniencing you.'

His sarcasm—so far removed from the friendly, smiling man she'd met a year ago—bit hard, ruffling her usually calm demeanour. Her chin shot up. 'Your plans are not inconveniencing *me* in the slightest, Mr Stanley. However, my expertise lies in nursing adults and therefore I may well inconvenience your patient.'

'For heaven's sake, I'm not asking you to play games with him.' He shoved his hand through his hair, the thick curls snagging at his fingers. 'Look, I need a plastics nurse who's good at her job. Either you fit the bill or you don't.'

'She definitely fits the bill,' Keri interrupted, her voice full of soothing tones as she threw Chloe a look that said, *What on earth is the matter with you?* 'Chloe will head up a team of three nurses to cover each block of twenty-four hours for as long as the child needs that level of care.'

Chloe gulped in a steadying breath to stop the simmer of panic that was threatening to take off into a full-blown boil. Nursing children wasn't something she did. Even as a student nurse she'd minimised her exposure with a bit of dumb luck. Rostered onto the children's ward during a flu epidemic, she'd ended up nursing more adults under the bright, owl-covered bedspreads than children. This time, however, her luck had run out.

Keri took Luke's arm and steered him towards the door. 'How are Anna and Amber? Happy to be back home in sunny Australia?'

Luke blanched, the little colour he had in his face completely draining away. 'You don't know?'

His quiet words sent a chill through Chloe.

'I don't think I do,' Keri said warily.

He looked out towards the ward, avoiding eye contact with the three of them. 'Anna died thirteen months ago.'

His pain jerked through Chloe and her fingers closed around her cup so hard it crumpled in her hand. The successful surgeon who'd once had everything had lost it.

Keri sagged against the doorjamb. 'I'm so sorry, Luke, none of us had any idea…'

'Now you do.' His words scorched the air like the summer sun—harsh, burning and devoid of any compassion that he'd just delivered shocking news. He turned abruptly to face Chloe, his emotions masked by tight control. 'Don't be late on Thursday.' Just as abruptly, he strode out of the ward.

At that moment Chloe would have given anything to avoid Thursday. As she absently listened to Kate and Keri express their stunned sorrow for Luke, the ramifications of the next few days—weeks even—hit her. The man with the reputation of being fun, forgiving and easy to work with had totally vanished. In his place was a tortured and grieving soul with a personality as black as his jet hair.

It was a hell of a way to start her thirty-first year.

CHAPTER TWO

'HOW WAS SHE today?' Luke asked, sitting at his sister's outdoor table under the protective shadow of a huge shade sail and watching Amber running around the yard with her older cousins. He tried not to think about the fact he had to take her home to a quiet and empty house.

'The kids ran her ragged and she napped for three hours straight,' Steph said with an apologetic shrug. 'I guess that means she'll be hard to settle tonight. Sorry.'

He thought about the hard-fought routine he'd established with his toddler daughter, all of which was about to change now he was returning to full-time work. 'Hopefully, she's running off more energy now and will snuggle down at seven.'

His sister gave him a contemplative glance. 'So, how was it?'

'What?' He was being deliberately obtuse just in case his perceptive sister was having an off day.

'Being back at Gold Coast City?'

The memory of the shocked expression of the nurses slugged him. 'They didn't know.'

'Hell.' Her hand touched his arm.

'Yeah.' He stirred the ice at the bottom of his glass. 'I thought someone would have told them. I mean, hospitals are usually seething with gossip, rumour and innuendo, but just when I needed my personal life to be part of that mill, it wasn't.'

'I guess because it happened in France...'

'Maybe.' He drained his glass, trying not to think of that night when the gendarmes had told him his car had drifted onto the wrong side of the road. 'I had to tell them, Steph. I had to watch their horror and then their sympathy. God, I thought by now I was over having to tell people. I thought at least that part would be done.'

'It'll get easier.'

'Don't say that.' He glared at her, hating platitudes. He'd heard enough of them to know they only made the speaker feel better. Nothing was ever going to make him feel better. Nothing could erase the bald fact that he'd unwittingly killed his darling wife.

Steph's usually smiling mouth flattened. 'We'll *always* miss Anna. You know I meant walking into the hospital and talking with the staff will get easier. Try to look on the plus side. By the time you return on Thursday they'll have digested the news and be onto something else. Besides, given the turnover of staff, half of them probably don't even know you.'

The image of a pair of hazel eyes framed by black-rimmed glasses, followed by a mane of glossy, chestnut hair, pinged into his mind. Eyes that seemed familiar and yet he felt sure that he'd never met the nurse before. If they'd met, he'd have remembered that particular combination of khaki-green flecked with brown. He knew that grief screwed with memory and his had been bad lately but, even so, she hadn't shown any spark of recognition either. Hell, he really didn't know why he was even thinking about her.

He tried to stop the picture of her at those eyes but, like a movie reel, his brain recalled way more. In vivid detail, it rolled over her round, smiling face, her ruby-red lips that peaked in a delectable bow and her lush curves that no uniform could hide. Natural curves that in a bygone era women had embraced but which today so many tried to dominate into submission. Curves that said, *I am all woman.*

His mouth dried as the same short, sharp kick of arousal he'd experienced the first time he'd seen her stirred again. He rubbed the back of his neck. God, what was wrong with him? Anna had only been dead just over a year and he missed her every single day. He didn't want to look at other women, let alone lust after them.

'You okay, Luke?'

No. 'Yep.' He didn't like the inquiring look in his sister's eyes so he shifted conversational gears. 'The daycare centre called and they can take Amber for the extra days each week while you're away on your big trip.'

Relief flitted across Steph's face. 'That's good news. Of course, if you hadn't sold the house around the corner...'

He shook his head, thinking about the five-bedroom house with its indoor-outdoor living, swimming pool and a spectacular view of the tidal canal and its constant boat traffic.

He and Anna had bought the colonnaded home when he'd been appointed to Gold Coast City. It was the place they'd taken Amber home to from the hospital and settled her into her nursery with the crooked wallpaper frieze of pastel balloons that he'd put on the wall. Anna had taken one look at his dodgy handiwork and had teased him not to give up his day job.

'I couldn't live in that house, no matter how close it was to you, and besides…' he raked his hand through his hair '…it's moot in this instance because you're going to be gone for two months. I appreciate that you've been having Amber three days a week while I've been doing some private practice stuff, but I don't want you putting your life on hold for me. Marty's been talking about driving up the centre from Adelaide to Darwin for as long as I've known him, and it isn't fair to you, him or the girls to put it off again.'

'Luke, we're family and we help each other out. It's what families do. And the moment we get back I want to have Amber three days a week again.' She leaned closer to him and smiled. 'We love having her here, and the girls have stopped pestering me for a baby brother or sister so it's win-win.'

He tried to match her smile. 'No more baby plans, then?'

'No. Marty wanted two and I wanted four so we've compromised on three.'

Luke detected a wistfulness in his sister's voice, but before he could say anything Amber took a tumble on the grass and sent up a shriek of shocked surprise.

'Up you get, honey,' Luke called out as he rose to his feet and crossed the lawn. He swung his daughter into his arms and gave her knees and elbows a quick inspection for skin damage but could only see grass stains. He kissed her. 'Bath time for you, young lady.'

'Play ducky?' Amber asked hopefully.

'Play ducky in your bathtub,' Luke replied, bracing himself for a howl of disappointment that Amber had to leave her beloved cousins and come with him.

'Okay.'

'Okay.' He kissed her again, battling a surge of sadness for them both. 'Let's go…' He couldn't bring himself to say home because the cottage was just a house.

Chloe checked little Made's observations as the six-year-old slept. The white of the sheets and pillowcases made his black hair and deeply olive skin seem even darker, and in the big hospital bed he looked tiny and in need of protection. Her protection.

She bit her lip against the rush of emotions—some caring, some painful, most tinged with loss. She'd lost her baby and along with it her chance to be a mother. Self-preservation meant she'd chosen not to nurse children, and in her off-duty life, while she didn't technically avoid children, she didn't actively seek them out either.

She knew from bitter experience that letting her mind drift backwards was unwise and unhealthy so she drew on every ounce of her professionalism. *He's a patient, like all your other patients.*

She picked up the Bahasa-English dictionary

she'd purchased and thumbed through the pages. Last night she'd recalled her basic Indonesian from primary school, and using the dictionary she'd looked up the words for pain and thirst, adding them to her small list of phrases. The little boy's mother spoke less English than Chloe spoke Bahasa, which wasn't saying much, so the dictionary was getting a good workout.

Between them, they were muddling along and Made was pain-free, which right now was the most important thing for his recovery.

Chloe stifled a yawn. It had been a long day and she still had an hour to go before her relief took over. She'd started her shift early due to Luke Stanley's request that she attend the operation. She'd arrived before him and had spent the time chatting with the anaesthetist about Made's post-operative pain relief while the rest of the theatre staff had scurried around, getting ready. The scout nurse had set up Mr Stanley's favourite playlist of music but the moment he'd walked briskly into Theatre he'd demanded it be turned off.

The mood of the room had instantly changed—

people had become tentative and quiet. Eyes had flashed and flickered over the tops of surgical masks, sending coded messages to each other. Luke Stanley had operated almost silently, his only words being infrequent curt demands for instruments that the experienced scrub nurse had failed to anticipate, and as a result the air was thick with confused tension. People wanted to be sympathetic and understanding, but nothing about Luke Stanley's demeanour allowed it.

Initially, Chloe hadn't understood why Luke had insisted she be in the operating room, but it had been utterly hypnotic watching him in action and seeing how those long, strong and competent fingers had freed the thick, scarred adhesions on Made's neck. He deserved his reputation as a talented surgeon and his skills were restoring little Made's life to normality. The young boy would once again be able to turn his head, and in time he would once again enjoy playing child-hood games.

Although it hadn't been absolutely necessary to attend the operation to be able to nurse Made effectively, knowing exactly what Luke Stanley had done, seeing from where the skin grafts had been taken and how they had been positioned, did help. She rechecked Made's analgesia drip and then set about her fifteen-minute routine of observing the skin grafts. Circulation was key and she wanted to see pink, warm skin, not white and cool skin.

'How's he doing?'

Surprised, Chloe spun around at the sound of Luke's deep but curt voice. Just like their first encounter fifteen months ago, she hadn't heard him enter the ward—only this time her hands were thankfully empty. This time Luke's face wasn't open, smiling and cheerful. Instead, gaunt skin stretched over high cheekbones, giving him a haunted look.

'He's doing great,' she said, suppressing a shudder at the pain Luke wore like a greatcoat. Her brain sought for something she could say that could give them a shared connection, which might make him look less formidable and unapproachable. 'Do you always enter the room panther style?'

His dark brows drew down. 'What are you talking about?'

She ignored his brusqueness and tried a smile. 'You have a habit of entering a room silently and surprising me.'

He looked blank and utterly uncomprehending. 'This is the first time I've seen you with a patient.'

She shook her head. 'Just before you went to France, you walked into this same ward very quietly and gave me such a fright that I covered you in iodine.'

His vivid green eyes finally flashed with recognition. 'Chloe? Nick's sister?' He said the words as if he needed to hear them to cement them in his mind.

'That's right. Lucky for you that today my hands are empty,' she joked.

He glanced down at his scrubs, as if he couldn't remember what he was wearing, and then shrugged his wide shoulders like it really didn't really matter anyway. 'If there's any change with Made's grafts, notify me immediately. You have my mobile number?'

She swallowed a sigh. So much for attempting a friendly connection with the man. 'I do. Are you leaving the hospital now?'

He seemed to stiffen. 'Yes. I have to pick my daughter up from daycare. They don't like it when I'm late.'

'I don't suppose she likes it either.'

His eyes burned, emitting sparks of green. 'You think I want Amber in daycare ten hours a day? She doesn't have a choice and neither do I.'

The loud and terse words slammed into her like a punch to her solar plexus, making her heart race.

Made's mother startled from her nap in the chair. *'Apa yang salah?'* Mrs Putu asked anxiously.

Chloe didn't need to understand the words to know that the mother was stressing that Luke's raised voice meant something was wrong with her son. She reached out her hand to comfort and reassure the woman.

'Semuabaik,' Luke said softly. 'All is well.'

'Terimakasih, Dokter.' The woman visibly relaxed and sank back in her chair.

Chloe turned back to face Luke, surprised at the ease in which the foreign language had rolled off his tongue but furious with him for upsetting Mrs Putu. For deliberately misconstruing her own words. Adrenaline pelted through her, sending rafts of agitation jetting along her veins, and she needed to work extra-hard to appear calm.

Choosing her words carefully, she shepherded Luke towards the door. 'I'm not judging you about daycare,' she said, *sotto voce*, 'I was talking about the fact your daughter probably doesn't like it when you're late either.'

He stared down at her, his jaw tight, his height dwarfing her by a good thirty centimetres, and she caught the scent of his spicy cologne. His eyes, which at times could be bright green, were now a dark moss and filled with so many flickering emotions that it was hard to decode any of them over and above the dominant and glaring pain.

Tall, dark, gorgeous, brooding and tortured.

Her heart did a ridiculous leap, which had absolutely nothing to do with his indignation or her chagrin.

Oh, no, she told herself sternly. *The man is grieving and you do not need to rescue him. You've just got your own life back on track. You've got a dog to love and be loved by.*

Shimmering tingles taunted her, spinning through her with their intoxicating call. *But it's been so long...*

No way in hell, Chloe! her ever-vigilant internal guard yelled. *Keep it simple, remember?*

She sucked in a long, deep breath, trying desperately to banish the delicious buzz of addictive warmth. 'Everything's fine here, Mr Stanley. Go and get your daughter.'

His eyes widened at her dismissal of him, and he rubbed his forehead with his fingers and his temple with his thumb as if his head hurt. 'Goodnight, then.'

She watched him turn and leave without giving an apology and she tried not to let it rankle. After all, it shouldn't bother her one bit because she was used to working with surgeons who believed all should bow down before them and kiss their feet. She also knew that apologies for bad behaviour were few and far between. Only

Luke Stanley had always been an exception to that rule.

His reputation for skill and good humour had always meant that people had fallen over themselves to work with him. The nursing and auxiliary staff, from cleaners to occupational therapists, had loved him, and whenever he'd put together a team to go to Asia or Africa for a six-week stint with the foundation, repairing cleft lips and palates, there had always been more applicants than positions.

That man had utterly disappeared when his wife had died.

She wasn't a stranger to grief, and she understood the pain of it all too well. She'd been lost in the midst of it once, for a year, floundering in the suffocating darkness that had become both enemy and friend. It had been her beloved brother Nick who'd hauled her unwilling teenage mind out of the black and treacherous morass and pushed her back into the light of life.

At the time it had hurt like nothing she'd ever experienced before or since and the battle not to let grief become a toxic legacy had been beyond hard, but she'd done it. Years later, when Jason had told her he wouldn't marry her because she couldn't give him a child, she'd teetered on the edge but she'd survived and learned. Today, she knew that even though her life now wasn't anything like that she'd imagined for herself as a naïve sixteen-year-old, and neither was it the life she truly wanted, it was a life worth living and living well.

You could show him how to do it.

The thought clanged loudly in her head like the penetrating sound of a fire alarm and she wished she could put noise-cancelling headphones over her brain.

Yes, she was a nurse, a member of a caring profession, and, yes, she had the ability to recognise when someone needed help. Luke Stanley definitely fell into that category—he needed help big-time—but she was also a survivor. Helping a grieving man with a child would be more harmful to her than helpful to him and she wasn't prepared to risk her hard-won stability.

No, it wasn't her job to do the 'hands-on' helping stuff with Luke Stanley, but she'd talk to Keri and Kate. After all, they knew Luke a hell of a lot better than she did.

CHAPTER THREE

'WANT BUNNY,' AMBER sobbed into Luke's shoulder, her tears making a damp patch on his cotton shirt.

'Hello, Amber, I'm Mr Clown,' Luke said in a voice he thought might sound like a clown's as he waggled the soft toy near his daughter's face.

Amber's hand knocked the clown sideways. 'Want bunny!'

Luke's head pounded with fury at himself and despair for Amber, which rumbled through him and reminded him he had so much to learn as a father. How had he forgotten to check that her beloved bunny had been in the backpack when he'd collected Amber from daycare?

Because you were thinking about Chloe Kefes.

His anger at himself was buried deep with sharp roots. How had he forgotten ever meeting her? Unlike most of his colleagues, he didn't forget names and faces, especially when there was another connection, like her being Nick's sister. But today he'd needed all her prompting to recall the iodine incident.

He hated that he'd forgotten as much as he hated the fact his mind kept repeating the way her plump lips curved into a smile. A generous, captivating smile, which dimpled her round cheeks and danced in her eyes. A smile that had faded under the onslaught of his bitter words—words generated by his own self-loathing and hurled out to land on the nearest target. It wasn't Chloe's fault that Amber was motherless and in full-time daycare. No, that responsibility lay solely at his feet.

Amber's wails sounded even louder than before.

Damn it, he shouldn't still be thinking about Chloe. What sort of a pathetic excuse for a father was he?

Poor Amber. She was rarely without her talisman bunny—her security blanket in her ever-changing world. Her one stable item in a confusing place, where her previously mostly at-home father was now absent during the day, and her aunt, uncle and cousins were unexpectedly gone too.

He'd telephoned the director of the daycare centre, who, although sympathetic to his plight, had not been prepared to make the twenty-minute drive to open the building to retrieve the bunny, no matter what Luke had offered. The doctor in him understood. The father with the hysterical child wasn't quite so reasonable.

He lined up all Amber's cuddly toys. 'Look, honey, Teddy's sad and needs a cuddle,' he tried, desperate to turn the situation around.

Amber screamed.

Abandoning any attempts to try and settle her into her cot, Luke carried her outside to the deck. The slow and rhythmic roll of the waves hitting the sand boomed around them and the silver rays of moonlight beamed down through the streaks of cloud to sparkle on the Pacific Ocean. He lowered himself onto the sun lounger and settled Amber on his chest, his hand patting her sobbing and shuddering body and matching the beat to the tempo of the waves.

Oh, so very slowly, as the inky darkness cloaked them both, Amber's frantic sobs turned into occasional, gulping hiccoughs until her breathing steadied and her body relaxed against his. Despair finally turned to sleep. He knew he should probably take her into her room and settle her into her cot, but after the last hour he didn't dare move in case she woke up, remembered the missing bunny and was again faced with having to go through the same trauma.

He knew all about that. Even now, living in a different house, he still woke occasionally expecting to find Anna there, only to have the realisation she was gone dump all over him. Over and over. Anna was gone because he'd made a critical error that couldn't be fixed. At least Amber was spared the memory of missing her mother, or at least he hoped she was. She'd only been six months old when Anna had died. Did she miss someone she couldn't remember?

He pulled a beach towel off the chair next to him and covered both of them with it to ward off the slight chill of the night air. Amber may not have a mother, but she had a loving extended family who smothered her in love. Were aunts, uncles and cousins enough?

The image of clear and honest hazel eyes beamed into his brain and he instantly shut them out. He'd only ever had eyes for one woman, and even though Anna was gone he had no desire to look elsewhere. The idea was abhorrent to him. Closing his eyes, he found himself battling random images of dimples and long, glossy chestnut hair. Desperate, he focused on the sound of the sea and willed sleep to come.

The elevator doors closed and Callie Richards, neonatal specialist, wished she could turn off her pager and hide in the steel box for an hour. She knew it was just an idle dream, however, because the NICU was full of sickies and Nick Kefes, Gold Coast City's beloved obstetrician, had just called her, flagging a possible case that might require her skills. She hoped Nick was being his usual over-cautious self and that she might actually get home tonight to sleep in her own bed.

Who else's bed would you sleep in? Certainly not arrogant Cade Coleman's.

Shut up!

She hated how her conscience threw up unexpected reminders of her most stupid mistake to date—flirting outrageously with Cade Coleman. Just when she'd been convinced she'd successfully let go of the embarrassing memory, her brain did this to her. It made little sense because it wasn't like he was the only man she'd ever had practise forgetting. Truth be told, he was just one in a long line of men—men she rarely gave a second thought after she'd picked up her shoes and tiptoed quietly out their doors, never to see them again.

Correction—thinking about Cade made *no* sense because she hadn't even got to first base with him, thank God, let alone kissing and sex. But flirting with him had been a basic error—a rookie mistake she should be long past making.

Rule Number One: don't hit on the men you work with. Prior to Cade, she'd held fast to that rule like superglue because it meant she never had to deal with coming face to face with her folly on a daily basis.

Mind you, the man didn't seem perturbed by

that fact so she shouldn't be either and, damn it, she wasn't. Just yesterday she'd given him a polite nod and not felt a moment's regret. Well, not very much of a moment, anyway.

Emotionally stunted men like Cade are not worth thinking about. She repeated the mantra to herself.

The elevator pinged, the doors opened and she stepped out to see Chloe Kefes standing and staring through the large windows of the special care nursery. On the other side of the glass were the cots that were home to the premature babies who were now almost full term. The staff affectionately called this part of the room the 'fattening-up' corner and when babies graduated here, they were close to being discharged home into the loving care of their parents.

'Hi, Chloe, you're a long way from Plastics.'

The nurse looked momentarily flustered and a pink flush stained her cheeks. 'I'm on my way back from Pathology.'

'You're taking the long way, then.' Callie laughed, understanding exactly, because sometimes in a fraught and busy hospital, taking a circuitous route gave a professional the only breathing space they got in a day. She followed Chloe's gaze. Twin boys had managed to each get a hand out from under their bunny rug and their little fingers were exploring the air.

'Those two were so sick and now look at them. They're just itching to explore life,' Callie said with a glow of satisfaction.

'Hmm.'

Callie glanced at Chloe, who was usually a lot chattier. 'Tough day?'

Chloe shrugged. 'I used to love coming to work but for the last few weeks the ward's been on tenterhooks. It seems no matter what we do, we can't do anything right.'

'Luke Stanley?'

She nodded. 'When the consultant's not happy…'

'No one is.' Although Callie didn't know Luke, she'd heard the news of his wife's death on the hospital grapevine. She touched Chloe's arm in an understanding gesture because nurses often took the brunt of a doctor's unhappiness.

'When my day sucks, I often come down here

and look at the babies.' Callie smiled. 'There's something about them that makes you feel better and gives you hope, right?'

Chloe spun away from the window so fast that she almost knocked into her. 'I have to get back to work, Callie. Catch you later.'

She walked away before Callie had time to say another word. Astonished by the nurse's abrupt departure, she watched her disappear into the lift. Chloe was usually so upbeat—one of those people who seemed to be almost too bright, bubbly and good humoured to be real, although Callie knew her to be absolutely genuine. Chloe Kefes was one of the hospital's best nurses, with a perfect blend of professionalism, empathy and good cheer. For her to be so skittish, Luke Stanley must really be getting her down.

Men. Working with them should be straightforward but so often it was far from that. Thoughts of Cade threatened to rise but she cut them off at the knees. She'd made a fool of herself once and she had no plans to do it again. She was over and done with Cade Coleman.

She pushed open the door of the nursery and

did a round of her little patients. The baby with bronchomalacia, who was being nursed in the open cot, was improving and she hoped that by tomorrow he'd be breathing without the assistance of continuous positive airway pressure. She took the time to reassure anxious parents about the standard procedure of using an apnoea mattress with all premature babies, and she was thrilled to be able to help a mother hold her premature baby for the very first time.

Callie loved her job. Unlike her private life, here at the hospital she was in control and she knew exactly what she was doing. After she'd completed the discharge papers for the twins, Nick still hadn't called back, so she decided to grab something to eat while she had the chance.

As she reached the tearoom door, laughter and conversation rolled out to meet her.

'Oh, my God, that Cade Coleman has to be the sexiest man ever to walk the floor of this hospital.'

Callie recognised the voice of Sara Hennessey, one of the NICU nurses, and she stopped short of entering the room.

'I know, right? And that accent! He only has to say *hello* and I'm a puddle of lust,' replied a voice Callie wasn't familiar with.

'He is without a doubt *the* best addition to Gold Coast City in a very long time. I heard from the theatre nurses that Callie Richards—'

Oh, God, no! Callie hastily spun on her heel, away from the tearoom, and punched open the nursery door. It took every ounce of control she had to keep her feet from breaking into a run. One dumb mistake. It was bad enough she'd plastered herself all over him when they'd danced and then gone on to suggest that she was open to more, but to have the nursing staff talking about her was more than she could bear. She'd worked so hard at keeping her private life exactly that—private.

Never again was she going to give anyone any excuse to talk about her. From this day forward she was marking Cade Coleman and every other red-blooded male in the hospital as *off limits*.

'What is the point of writing down clear instructions if no one reads them?'

As Luke's terse words broke over Chloe like jagged shards of glass, she counted slowly to five. Despite talking with Keri and Kate and outlining her concerns about Luke, and their meeting with staff in Theatre to try and work out the best way to handle him, not much had changed in two weeks. With Keri and Kate, with whom he'd worked before, he seemed to hold himself in check, but there were still moments when he was difficult, and on those occasions he took down everyone in his path.

Oh, why had Keri gone to a seminar today, leaving her in charge of the ward? Now she had to deal with the man she'd nicknamed *the panther*. Like the big black cat, he was a perfect specimen—sleek, muscular and strong. At times his emerald eyes would glow with ruthless keenness that made her shiver with delicious anticipation.

It unnerved her because she didn't want to be attracted to him. She didn't want to be attracted to *any* man, let alone one who had a neon '*excess-baggage*' sticker plastered all over him. That would be like throwing herself under a truck—both dangerous and deadly to her peace of mind.

Stay strong. Remember, no man is for you, especially not this one.

A raft of heady need skipped through her, deaf to her entreaties, and she stomped on it hard. She didn't even like this version of Luke, so why was her body doing this to her? When he was in one of his moods, he pounced on any weakness, attacking first and pausing second. Yes, the man was grieving, and for the last couple of weeks the staff had been making allowances for him, but that didn't absolve him from basic manners.

Glancing up at his handsome but scowling face, she said, 'And hello to you, Mr Stanley. Welcome to Ward Six.'

'Chloe.' He gave her a stiff nod as if he recognised that he should have at least greeted her first before lobbing his complaint at her like a grenade. 'Mrs Wharton's drain tubes should have been removed today. The woman's been through breast cancer and the least she can expect is to be free of tubes so she can get an idea of how her new breasts are going to look.'

'I agree.'

'I don't need you to agree.' He rubbed his temple and squinted at her as if he was having trouble focusing. 'I just need the drain tubes out.'

'And they will come out.' In every encounter with the irascible consultant she'd needed to draw on her counselling skills. It was exhausting. 'As a result of your busy morning in the operating theatre, we're flat out here with post-op checks. Along with that, we're one nurse down and as I am sure you're aware you didn't specify an exact time for the removal. There's still a lot of today left.'

She smiled at him to reinforce her commitment. 'I guarantee you that the drain tubes will be out before I go off duty at three.'

'Good,' he said gruffly, scrawling an order on another patient's chart. 'Make sure they are.'

His response crossed her threshold of what she was prepared to have dished out to her. 'Mr Stanley…Luke.'

His silver pen stilled in his hand. 'Yes?'

'I may not be Keri and we may not have had a long working relationship but I'm good at my job. When I give you my word, know that it will be honoured. I'd appreciate being treated with the same professional respect that I accord you.'

Despite the semi-permanent dull ache behind his eyes, Luke felt Chloe's words strike him and strum a chord. God, when had he turned into such an ogre?

Since you killed your wife. The cancerous words spread their malignancy through him again, ramping up the hatred he held for him-self—an abhorrence he shielded Amber from. Like a full reservoir, there were times when it spilled out at work, no matter how hard he tried to contain it.

'I have a headache.' He rubbed his eyes and hid behind an excuse because it was easier than telling Chloe the truth.

Her hazel eyes widened in disbelief at his jus-tification for rudeness, which even sounded lame to his own ears.

'I'm sorry to hear that,' she said, her chin tilt-ing up defiantly, 'but is there any need to inflict it on us? Here...' She fished a foil disc out of her pocket. 'Take some ibuprofen.'

He accepted the two white tablets along with

the admonishment and tried a wry smile. 'Spoken like a true nurse.'

Her lush mouth softened into a smile and the stirrings of warmth that eddied in him each time he met her became waves of liquid heat. Then she laughed and the sound surfed on the heat, pulling up memories of the times he'd laughed easily. For a brief moment the constant reminders of why he didn't laugh much any more—why he didn't feel any more—faded away and he let the wondrous and glorious sensations of life surge through him.

Betrayer.

Guilt seared him like the dry heat from a furnace, sucking the oxygen from the joy until it shrivelled to nothing. He didn't deserve to feel happy. He wanted to turn and leave—march away from Chloe immediately. Away from the temptation that represented everything he could no longer have in his life.

You have to work with her.

He did, and it wasn't Chloe's fault that Anna was dead. It wasn't Chloe's fault that with one ill-timed action he'd screwed up his perfect life.

He stood facing her with his fingers clenched on his Swiss pen and tried to apologise. 'I do appreciate your work here, Chloe.'

'Thank you.'

This time her smile made her dimples and her eyes dance, and the treacherous heat flared again, filling him with longing before vanishing and leaving only bitterness. Hell, he couldn't cope with this roller-coaster ride of emotions every time he came to the ward, but he could hardly ask Administration to have her removed. A thought struck him—the perfect solution for six weeks or more.

'You did a great job with Made, so great, in fact, that I think you should sign up for the foundation's cleft palate tour that leaves next week.' He tried for what he hoped was a reassuring smile. 'Jenny Patrick's looking for people and you're a natural with kids.'

She flinched as if he'd struck her. 'I appreciate the compliment but that won't be possible.'

No. 'Why not?' He heard the bark in his voice and wished he could snatch the words back because, damn it, his fear sounded the same as anger.

She blinked at him as if she couldn't believe he'd asked her the question. 'Because…' Her cheeks flamed red and she twirled her ponytail tightly around her forefinger as if she was struggling to give a reason. 'Because it's just *not* possible.' She picked up Glenda Wharton's drug chart and slapped it against his chest. 'Please write up some milder analgesia for her and I'll take out the drain tubes now.'

Her expression—a combination of defiance and pain—was all too familiar and it silenced him. As much as he didn't want to have to see Chloe every day, he didn't want to hurt her either. While he quickly wrote the order across the page, neither of them said another word.

He got the distinct feeling both of them were battling demons they wanted to keep secret.

CHAPTER FOUR

'HE SHOULD SLEEP all afternoon because I ran him halfway to Burleigh Heads this morning,' Chloe told Nick as she settled Chester into his basket inside a playpen.

Even though Lucy had taken the twins to visit a friend, Chloe didn't want the puppy to escape and cause her sister-in-law any more work. Being the mother of twins was enough to exhaust her, without adding anything extra. Despite today being Chloe's weekend off, the hospital had called, asking if she could come in for three hours. She was happy to work but her puppy was still too small to be on his own for more than an hour.

'You'll be fine with your uncle, won't you?' Nick fondled the pup's golden ears.

'Enjoy him, because he's as close to a nephew as you're ever going to get.'

The acrid words spewed out of her, shocking

her. For years she'd kept a tight lid on her sorrow, and she wasn't sure why today it had momentarily lifted, especially with her brother. He was the *one* person who knew the details of what had happened to her all those years ago at sixteen. If it hadn't been for Nick and his quick actions, she'd be dead.

Nick's eyes, the identical colour to hers, darkened with concern. 'You okay?'

'I will be.' She forced a smile. 'I think turning thirty was harder than I thought.'

'It can be a tough birthday,' Nick said, still patting the dog.

'Oh, yeah.' It had been a tough couple of weeks in so many ways—her birthday, working with Luke Stanley and nursing the little Balinese boy. She'd even added to it by walking past the special care nursery, instead of avoiding it like she normally did. For an extra dose of agony she'd paused, gazing at the babies. Reminding herself of what she could never have.

'You know, Chester reminds me of Cerberus,' Nick said, his voice filled with surprise.

'Sorry.' Chloe bit her lip, thinking about their

childhood dog. When their strict Greek father had discovered she'd broken his draconian rules and had snuck out of the house to meet a boy, he'd punished her by having the dog put down. Her actions had cost Nick his beloved dog. 'I think that's why I chose him.'

'Don't let your mind go back to that toxic place, sis. *Baba* just wanted an excuse to get rid of the dog, and if it hadn't happened then it would have happened another time.' Nick rose to his feet and gave her a hug. 'You really are having a tough time, aren't you?'

'Just a bit.' She pulled back from her brother. 'I'd better get going. At least Luke Stanley won't be in today to upset everyone, so that's something.'

'Give the guy a break, Chloe,' Nick admonished gently.

She slung her leather backpack over her shoulder with a jerk. 'He's mostly fine with Keri and Kate and I've done my best to be understanding, but there are times when he's tough to work with.'

'There's no time limit on grief.'

'You're preaching to the converted, Nick. Say *hi* to Lucy and the twins for me.'

He grinned at the mention of his wife and children. 'Will do. And, Chloe…'

She paused at the door. 'Yes?'

'Keep looking forward. Promise?'

She nodded at their old mantra—the cluster of words that had kept them strong through difficult times. 'Will do.'

Closing the door behind her, she walked the short distance to the hospital. Accident and Emergency was seething with humanity on this fine and sunny Saturday afternoon and she signed in, introducing herself to the staff.

'There are two rugby players with concussion and head lacerations who've just arrived,' said Greg Lindall, the nurse-in-charge. 'I've called Plastics and someone will be down.'

'I'm on it.' She pushed her arms into a gown, grabbed some dressing packs and made her way to the cubicles. Two burly men, their toned and buff bodies dwarfing the hospital trolleys, sat holding icepacks to their heads.

'Hi, I'm Chloe.'

'Finn Hudson,' replied one of the men.

'Harry Jameson,' said the other.

Chloe flicked through the head-injury charts that the ambulance officers had commenced and saw their ages. 'So, guys, your chart says you've both had concussion twice before. Isn't it time to give up the game?' She flicked on her pencil torch and checked Harry's pupils.

'We're thirty-two, not dead,' he said, flinching as she inspected the nasty gash on his head.

'That may be, but serial concussions are serious. You don't want to be forty and suffering from memory loss. What about taking up tennis?'

The guys stared at her as if she'd just suggested they take up floristry. She laughed. 'Okay, then, maybe not tennis, but there are plenty of other non-contact sports to challenge you. Cycling or kayaking. I do sea kayaking and it's fabulous.'

'If you're offering a lesson I might just consider it,' Finn said, his face breaking into a flirty grin.

She laughed, comfortable with the banter. She was used to male patients flirting with her, and she enjoyed the safety of it because it never led anywhere, which was just how she liked it.

'I'm going to stitch up the gash on your head now, Harry, but the cut close to your eye needs the expertise of the plastic-surgery registrar.'

'Yeah, like he had such a pretty boy face to begin with,' Finn teased.

'Mate, I wasn't the one spending the bucks ordering face cream online,' Harry shot back.

Chloe listened to their nonsense as she carefully shaved a small section around the head gash and cleaned it, before administering local anaesthetic to numb the area. She loved the routine of suturing—the way the curved needle brought the skin edges neatly together, the looping of the silk over the scissors and then the sharp snip to end the stitch. The skin edges joined cleanly and she was applying a dressing when Greg stuck his head through the gap in the curtains.

'Got a minute?'

'Sure.' She stripped off her gloves. 'Back in a minute, fellas.'

She followed Greg, swooshing the curtains closed behind her. 'What's up?'

Greg inclined his head towards the corridor that led to the tearoom.

Luke Stanley stood in the doorway—tall, dark and definitely handsome in his stormy, angst-ridden way.

Delicious shock waves of delight scudded through her, fast followed by dismay. Why couldn't she get a better handle on this crazy re-action to him?

He was holding a little girl whose black curly hair was identical to his own. *His daughter.* She snuggled in close to his broad chest, seeking sanctuary, and she clutched a soft toy tightly as if it would ward off the confusion of the com-bined sights and sounds of a busy A and E.

Luke's not rostered on.

A thousand questions bombarded her, starting with *Why is he here?* And followed by *Why on earth has he brought his daughter into a place that has the capacity to distress adults, let alone toddlers?*

The child didn't look sick, but then again Chloe's experience with children was so limited that she didn't trust her instincts at all.

Luke, his face a tight mask as usual, raised his free hand and motioned her over.

Mystified and somewhat hesitant, she made her way around the nurses' station and towards him. 'Is there a problem?'

'Yes.' Ragged exhaustion threaded through the words. 'Richard telephoned me half an hour ago. His car's broken down on the way back from Lamington National Park and the roadside service can't get him back here for at least three hours.'

Things started to make sense. 'So you're covering for him?'

He nodded slowly. 'Got it in one. He tells me there's a patient with a laceration close to an eye that needs suturing.'

Chloe glanced at the little girl, who was looking up at her from under half-lidded eyes. For Luke to suture, he was going to have to put the little girl down and someone was going to have to look after her while he did it.

Her mind leapt straight to the logical conclusion and lurched away from it so fast it almost gave her whiplash. 'I wish you'd called first because Mr Jameson's not strictly an emergency. He's on a head-injury chart for the next four hours so

Richard should be back in time to suture it. You and your daughter…'

'Amber,' he said quietly.

She swallowed. 'You and Amber are free to get back to enjoying your Saturday afternoon.'

He sighed, the sound weary and resigned. 'The three hours is only a ball park estimate, and seeing as I've woken Amber from her nap to get here, it's best I stitch it now rather than risk being called back later.'

And how are you going to do that? She refused to ask the obvious question and said instead in her best professional voice, 'I'll set up a suture trolley for you.'

'Thanks, but I can manage that on my own.' He smiled—only one of a very few true smiles she'd ever seen on his face—and it raced into those amazing, clear, green eyes of his, which were now fixed firmly on her.

Its effect was like a bomb detonating inside her, but instead of releasing shrapnel and carnage it was spinning out glorious, wondrous need that liquefied everything inside her. Her knees threatened to sag and she pressed her back up against the wall, seeking support.

This couldn't be happening. One smile should *not* do this to her.

You know better than this. He's difficult, unreasonable and a basket of pain.

Her body didn't care about protecting her heart and soul—it was too busy savouring every addictive whoosh of attraction. It wanted nothing more than to slide down the wall and fall panting at his feet. Better yet, have his hands touch her, his long fingers caress the hypersensitive skin under her arm and—

She fought every sensation, struggling to pull herself together and banish the surge of mind-altering lust that had just blindsided her.

'...minding Amber for me?'

The lust vanished the moment her brain decoded his question. *No, I can't do that.* 'But...' *Think!* '...she doesn't know me, and I'm on duty and...' Her voice trailed off as the smile faded from his eyes, replaced by something so stark it actually hurt her to look at it.

His body stiffened and he looked as if he might

shatter into a thousand pieces if anything brushed against him. 'I'm sorry to impose on you, Chloe. Please know that if I had any other option, I'd take it.'

The remote and prickly surgeon was firmly back in place. This time, though, she could see the bewildered man underneath the façade—the professional who knew he had a job to do vying with the father who was worried for his daughter. She recognised how much it had cost him to ask for her help.

She tried to say *no* to his request but her mouth refused to form the word. Despite the fact she'd normally wade through shark-infested waters to avoid spending time with children, it would be utterly heartless to refuse him. Instead, she found herself hauling in a fortifying breath.

'Sure,' she said. 'I can mind Amber.'

After all, how hard could it really be to mind a toddler for twenty minutes?

'I'm back,' Luke announced as he walked into the tearoom.

'Oh, good,' Chloe said with heartfelt emphasis.

He had the oddest sensation of things being totally back to front. He'd expected Amber to be the one counting down the minutes until he returned, but his daughter was quietly drawing, her head bent in concentration over a huge piece of paper. Chloe, on the other hand, was walking fast towards the door as if she couldn't get out of the room quickly enough. 'How did it go?'

'Fine.' She smiled but it didn't quite reach her eyes.

'Really? She can be pretty full on and she exhausts me. Sometimes I think a complicated piece of surgery is easier.'

A slow smile of relief crossed Chloe's face. 'Thank goodness. I thought it was just me. She was clinging onto her rabbit for dear life until I found the crayons and then she was a different child.'

He gazed at his beautiful daughter who was dealing with all sorts of experiences she wouldn't have had to had Anna still been alive. All he wanted for Amber was security, so that she'd grow up to trust and not be fearful of change, but it was a big ask, especially when he had to rely on the kindness of strangers.

Chloe Kefes is hardly a stranger.

He rubbed the back of his neck. 'In situations like this my sister would usually mind Amber but she's holidaying in central Australia. Thanks for helping me out, Chloe, I really appreciate it.'

'You're welcome.' She tilted her head quizzically, as if she was pondering something, and her ponytail swung out, the tips of her chestnut hair brushing against the soft skin of her neck. His fingers instantly itched, wanting to reach out and touch her—to dip into the hollow at her neck and then trail a path along her collarbone.

He quickly grabbed a mug off the bench, wanting to stop the feeling from going any further but at the same time not wanting her to leave. He'd been at home with Amber all day and he needed a conversation with an adult. 'Can I make you a tea or a coffee?'

She caught her bottom lip with her teeth. 'I should probably get back to work.'

He understood her prevarication. He'd hardly been easy to work with lately and he was probably the last person she wanted to chat with casually, but she'd helped him out and he wanted to make amends. Besides, sharing a coffee in the hospital tearoom with an almost-two-year-old chaperone was *the* safest place to chat with Chloe.

He rocked back on his heels. 'Greg said to tell you the rush is over for now and to take your time.' He saw her open her mouth to protest and he quickly cut her off with, 'I did the half-hour HIC check on Finn and Harry so you've got time. Besides, I know where they keep the stash of chocolate biscuits.'

'Chocolate?' Her eyes danced. 'Well, in that case, you've convinced me.'

'Biccy?' Amber looked up hopefully from her drawing.

'Yes, blossom, you can have one,' he replied, before looking back at Chloe. 'What's your drink of choice?'

She flicked out her thumb as if she was hitch-hiking. 'I'll have a latte if you're able to work that machine.'

He grinned, enjoying the feeling. 'Not only can

I work it, I totally dominate it. I did a barista course in Italy.'

Disbelief raced across her high cheeks. 'Seriously?'

'I'm not just a difficult plastic surgeon,' he offered by way of an apology.

'That's great to hear,' she said with a smile. 'I'm looking forward to seeing the different sides of you on the ward.'

No one had ever really taken him to task quite like this. Not his family. Not even Anna. 'Are you always this direct?'

She shrugged almost too easily, as if she was pushing something away. 'If I don't stand up for myself, no one else is going to.'

Her words dragged across his skin and something akin to sadness for her seeped in.

'Draw doggie more?' Amber held out the crayon to Chloe.

Chloe hesitated before moving slowly over to his daughter, almost as if she was forcing herself. Accepting the proffered crayon, she sat down next to Amber and quickly sketched a golden dog with big brown eyes. 'There you go, sweetie.'

'Chester.' Amber clapped.

'Chester?' Luke set down the latte with milk frothed to the perfect temperature in front of Chloe, wondering where Amber had learned the word.

'My new puppy.' Chloe sipped her coffee and her eyes drifted closed for a moment, before popping open again. 'Oh, my, you weren't just bragging, were you? You really can make coffee.'

Her astonishment made him laugh. 'There's no risk of me getting a big head around you, is there?'

'Not a chance.' She winked at him and then took another sip of her coffee, only this time her eyes stayed open. Behind the lenses of her glasses, bliss flared.

It was the bliss of the coffee but it caught him, cementing his gaze to hers and igniting the remnants of the heat he'd convinced himself he'd got under control. Heat that burst into flames of longing that licked parts of him he thought had died along with Anna. Should have died with Anna.

Every cell in his body yearned to touch her and his hand urged him to slide it over Chloe's and let his palm absorb her warmth and her energy. He imagined hearing her laugh again and just the thought streaked through him, making him feel alive—making him feel like a man again instead of a widower, a father and a responsible surgeon.

Hell, forget laughter, he wanted to kiss her— wanted to feel her body softly leaning into him and her curves melding to his. His lips would press against hers and then he'd feel hers yield so he could savour her heat, her essence and her taste. Did she taste like almonds and sunshine, like the scent of her hair? Or did she taste of the same hungry and desperate need that burned hot and vibrant inside him?

She gulped and the movement swooped down her neck and across her breasts. Breasts whose round, sweet curves defied any attempts to be rendered asexual behind her utilitarian uniform. Her body was one of curves, dips and swells, calling out to be cupped and traced and caressed by his hands, his mouth and his tongue.

His blood thundered through him—draining his brain and filling his groin, his heart pumping hard and spreading the intoxicating arousal into every cell of his body. Waking him up. Demanding he take action.

The scream of his need drowned out everything around him. Only Chloe existed, he was immune to everything else.

Chloe tried to haul air into her cramped lungs but the raging desire in Luke's eyes held her in its delicious grip. Tingling and throbbing need rushed her, sweeping through her, gaining volume, gaining intensity and control and crying out to be met. If she hadn't been sitting down her legs would have collapsed from under her as every cell gave in to the heady wonder of ecstasy.

Stop it. This is crazy.

She knew she had sexual needs but she'd learned the safe way to deal with them—on her own. Using a man to help her was so far from safe she refused to go there again. Jason had burned that lesson into her. Even with no emotional baggage, Jason, who had been reliable and easygoing, had proved to be dangerous to her heart and hazardous to her mental health. Getting involved with a rude and difficult traumatised widower with a child would be emotional suicide.

He's not always rude and difficult. You've caught glimpses of the man he was.

And, damn it, she had and that was the problem. This afternoon he'd made a real effort to be pleasant and she'd seen a different side of him. The Luke of previous weeks she could resist, but this Luke, the one who made coffee to die for, the one with the fire in his eyes that matched the burn of her body, left her wide open and without protection.

'Want to see Chester,' Amber announced loudly.

Luke's eyes widened so much that the inky black of his pupils almost obliterated the intense green. Lust vanished instantly, jolted out by shame and parental responsibilities. He swung his gaze away abruptly and focused on his daughter.

Relief flowed through Chloe, mixed with irrational disappointment. The moment of aberration for them both was over and she should be pleased.

I am pleased, she told herself firmly. Lust didn't belong in her life and, given the horrified expression on Luke's face ten seconds ago when his daughter had broken the moment, he didn't want it either.

'Want see Clo's doggie,' Amber said, as if she sensed neither of them had heard her the first time.

'Blossom, Chloe's puppy isn't here,' Luke said faintly.

'Where doggie?'

'At her house.'

Amber stood up. 'Let's go, Daddy.'

Luke looked as if he'd been hit over the head by a shovel. 'We can't go and see the dog, Amber.'

The little girl responded to the slightly sterner tone in her father's voice like a very normal toddler. She stamped her foot. 'Want to see puppy.'

'No.' Luke moved to pick up Amber but she ducked behind Chloe.

Chloe tried not to laugh at the child's determined antics, deciding that Amber's stubborn streak matched her father's. Right now he was looking utterly bewildered, confused and a just little bit cross. She felt a modicum of responsibility.

'I'm sorry, Luke. I showed her a photo of Chester when she was upset at you leaving. I don't have much experience with children and I didn't think she'd be so set on meeting him.'

He shook his head. 'You don't need to apologise. You're the one that helped out here.'

Chloe felt Amber's warm fingers pressing on the backs of her knees and something softened inside her. 'Will she be really upset if she doesn't meet him?'

Luke sighed. 'She has to learn she can't have everything her own way.'

'Doggie, woof-woof.'

'Yes, they say woof-woof,' Luke said, holding his hand out towards Amber.

Chloe's heart turned over. This little girl had stoically coped with being minded by a stranger in a strange place. And she'd been a tense stranger at that. She'd used the picture of Chester to help herself relax with Amber as much as to try to distract and entertain the child. Now all Amber wanted was to meet the puppy that Chloe had gushed and made so much of a fuss about. It seemed only fair to offer.

Don't do this. Even her father says she can't have everything her own way.

The entreaty in the little girl's eyes and the warmth of her hands on Chloe's legs tugged hard at her protective shell.

Do the right thing.

She pressed her thumbnail against her teeth, knowing how hard doing the right thing could be. 'Luke, emergencies aside, I'm off in about two hours. I'd be happy to show the p-u-p-p-y to A-m-b-e-r then, if that helps.'

Luke heard the offer and immediately felt trapped. Showing Amber the puppy meant spending more time with Chloe, and after that moment of insane electricity that had buzzed between them across the table, he didn't trust himself. God, what the hell was happening to him? He'd been rock-hard and lusting after a woman in front of his daughter.

A woman who wasn't Anna.

Guilt slugged him and the faint nausea that had been with him on and off for months rolled again in his gut. Amber would inevitably survive the disappointment of not seeing the puppy but did she deserve that just because he'd lost control of himself?

Yes.

No.

Maybe.

He closed his eyes against the stress-induced silver spots that danced into his vision, knowing exactly what he had to do and not wanting to do it.

CHAPTER FIVE

'CHESTER'S WORN HER out.' Chloe tilted her head towards Amber, who'd fallen asleep on her father's chest, her inky curls pressed flat against his polo shirt. The child looked serenely cute and adorable, which she was, and Chloe felt the familiar lump build in her throat whenever she thought about her childless life.

Don't go there.

'Really? Chester's worn her out?' Luke said, rolling his eyes before glancing over at the puppy, who was snoring gently, snuggled up on one of Amber's old baby blankets inside a broccoli box that he'd found for him.

He grinned. 'I think it may have been the other way around.'

Chloe laughed. 'Either way, they're both out for the count.'

Amber and the puppy had run non-stop for an

hour and then, as the sun had started to set, both had zonked out cold, which was how she'd come to be sitting with her legs tucked up under her on Luke's couch in his cottage. She stifled a yawn and caught Luke smiling at her.

'Sun and surf are a lethal combination,' she justified as she tried not to let his smile do dangerously delicious things to her. 'All those positive ions.'

He laughed. 'More like two thirty-somethings being out of condition and run ragged by a toddler and a puppy.'

'Hey, speak for yourself.'

His jet brows rose. 'Someone's a bit defensive about turning thirty.'

She didn't know his age but she guessed he was four or five years older than her. 'Did you find it hard?'

His eyes darkened and the humour in his face faded. 'Believe me, Chloe, there are much worse things in life than turning thirty.' He rose abruptly—suddenly swaying violently.

Chloe shot to her feet and grabbed his arm to

steady him and protect the sleeping child. 'Are you okay? Sit down before you drop Amber.'

He leaned against her for a moment, the weight making her stagger slightly until she widened her stance. 'Luke?'

He stared at her blankly, as if he hadn't heard her.

'Are you dizzy? Is it postural hypotension?' she asked, flipping through the most likely possibilities.

He blinked quickly, as if he was clearing his vision, and shock flared in his eyes. He straightened up fast, keeping Amber pressed close. Everything about him screamed *man protecting motherless child*.

'I'm fine,' he said briskly. 'There's wine in the fridge and some cheese and dips if you want to throw them on a plate while I settle Amber into her cot.'

She watched him walk away, surreptitiously checking his balance, but he was very steady on his feet and his gait devoid of any rolling motion. The dizziness must have been a combination of rising too fast and grief, given he'd probably been thinking about the death of his wife.

A moment before he'd stood up she'd wanted to say, *I know there are worse things than turning thirty. Some of them have happened to me too.*

Fortunately, that moment had passed and she hadn't voiced the thoughts. Self-disclosure rarely ended well and she had to work with Luke so, just like with her other colleagues, she planned to keep her past very much to herself.

His invitation to stay for a drink had been un-expected and the sensible thing to do would be to make her excuses, take Chester and drive home to her apartment. Her empty, rented apartment.

Luke's house—it was really a tiny cottage—was nestled in a small enclave of rainforest gar-den. With the beach at its front and the lush environs of wild, green tropical plants at its back, it seemed like a step back in time to the old Gold Coast. The Gold Coast that had existed before the glitz, glass and steel skyscrapers of today. Being so different and quaint, it should hum with warmth, but the walls were bare of any artwork or decorations. Her apartment in comparison suddenly didn't seem as quiet or as empty.

The only photo in the open-plan room was of a strikingly beautiful woman with blue eyes, blonde hair and a wide smile.

Chloe would stake her life it was a picture of Luke's wife, Anna. She quickly looked away, feeling like an elephant in comparison to the svelte and designer-dressed woman. *Comparisons were odious*, she quickly reminded herself, and there was no need for them anyway. Luke, with his wedding ring welded firmly on his finger, was obviously still very much in love with his wife.

If there was one thing Chloe knew about herself, it was that no man could love her. She had a list of examples starting with her father and ending with Jason. However, despite knowing all that, there was this *thing* that hovered between her and Luke. She knew she shouldn't stay around and explore it, but today at work, and now over the last hour, he'd made her laugh and smile and she'd enjoyed herself.

Was it so bad to want more of the same?

She pulled open the fridge door, pleased to see a bottle of her favourite *sauvignon blanc*, but as she slid it from the shelf she couldn't see any cheeses or dips. She bent her knees, turned her head and even moved some things around with her left hand but all she could find was a container of black olives and, more surprising, a packet of potato chips.

She took them both out, found some bowls to decant them into and then poured the wine. She was just returning the bottle to the fridge when Luke appeared. She handed him a drink.

'Thanks.' He frowned at the contents of the bowls. 'Couldn't you find the cheese?'

'There isn't any. Maybe you've eaten it already?'

'No, I only bought it this morning.' He put down his glass and opened the fridge door, looked inside and then closed it, confusion clear on his face. 'I don't get it. I was in that new deli down on Palm Avenue and while Amber was busy eating all the samples I bought some Brie, some blue vein and that gorgeous crumbly stuff from Tassie. So where is it?' He sorted through a pile of green shopping bags and then rubbed his temples.

She'd noticed he did that a lot and recalled his dizzy spell. 'Do you have a headache?'

'Hmm?' He looked up distractedly. 'Sorry, what?'

'You were rubbing your temples and I wondered if you had another headache.'

'Not a headache. More like a dull throb from being too hungry.'

'Have some chips.' She passed them over with a smile.

He touched one. 'Why are they cold?'

'They were in the fridge.'

This time he dropped his face into his hands before pushing his fingers through his hair with a long sigh. 'I tell you, shopping and unpacking with a toddler is obviously enough to make me lose my mind.'

He looked so weary and woebegone that she reached out and briefly touched his arm. 'Amber's like a rechargeable battery. She's either totally full on and claiming all of your attention or she's fast asleep. A bit like Chester, really.'

She laughed at the comparison despite the fact that being with the puppy was a lot more straight-forward than being with Amber and much less fraught with emotions. Spending time with the child was like being on a roller-coaster. There were moments of joy and fun and troughs of abject floundering and sadness.

'Luke, I've been known to come off night duty, buy groceries and leave half of them behind in the supermarket.'

'Now you're just trying to make me feel better,' he said with a slow smile.

The addictive warmth she got every time his eyes crinkled at the edges—taking away the pervading sadness that always circled him—glowed again. 'Is it working?'

'I think it is.' He took a long sip of his wine and studied her intently. 'I'm famished. I'd offer to cook for you but that would probably be an insult to all your great help today. How do you feel about take-out Malaysian satay from Mr Megat's?'

'Don't feel you have to feed me.'

'Well, I need food and you're welcome to join

me,' he said with a shrug, before picking up his mobile phone. 'Are you in or do you have to dash home for a hot date?'

She laughed loudly at the improbability of that.

'I'm surmising from your mirth that your social life is as exciting as mine.' He texted the food order and grabbed the bowl of chips.

She glanced at the photo of Anna, trying to decode if there was anything more to this invitation than to share food. 'Do you want a social life?'

His gaze followed hers and he flinched. 'Anna filled the weekends with events, and after a busy week I wasn't always thrilled to have to go out.'

'But now life seems quiet?'

'Chillingly so.'

She thought about how her life had changed dramatically at sixteen when she'd discovered she was pregnant. How the experience and eventual fall-out had put her in a different realm of understanding from her peers. 'Have the invitations dried up?'

He stared out of the large windows towards the horizon. 'People feel uncomfortable around me.'

'And you don't make it easy for them.'

His head swung around sharply and indignation duelled with admiration on his face. 'You really don't pull any punches, do you?'

Her shoulders rose and fell. 'Am I wrong?'

'I want to say yes but I can't.'

He was standing so close to her that his heat and scent of spicy musk spun through her nostrils. His hypnotic eyes with their mix of grief and pain hooked hers and he slowly reached out his fingers, tucking some stray strands of hair behind her ear.

'What's made you so scarily perceptive, Chloe Kefes?'

His touch shot through her like an electric shock—sparking and zinging bliss into every cell. Raising her hand, she pressed her palm against his cheek, feeling the rough scrape of stubble. She wanted to extend her touch—run her fingers across his silver-streaked temples, bury them in his hair and pull his head down to hers. She wanted the burn of his lips on hers.

The haunted look deep in his eyes stopped her cold.

Her hand fell away. He didn't want her to kiss

him. She stepped back, putting distance between them, and swallowed the hurt. Forcing a laugh to break the tension, she said, 'If I told you the secret of my perceptiveness, I'd have to kill you.'

Luke laughed—a real, deep, full-bellied chuckle that wrapped around her with the comforting caress of relief and the scratch of regret.

'Perceptive and dangerous,' Luke quipped as he fought his desire to kiss her. 'Remind me never to cross swords with you.' His body wanted her in his arms so desperately that his muscles ached, but his head and heart told him otherwise. He could feel Anna's gaze on him, radiating from the photo across the room. Added to that, Chloe's abrupt stepping back and her tight expression had clearly said, *Don't kiss me.*

Good. At least they were on the same page.

Neither of them wanted to act on this crazy heat that sizzled between them. Hell, neither of them wanted it to exist. Surely knowing that had to help.

You think?

He shouldn't have invited her for dinner but it

had seemed such a natural progression after their pleasant afternoon together.

You like her.

Yes, he'd concede that. He'd certainly enjoyed her company and the hour on the beach with her and the puppy. Watching both of them chase Amber and being chased back had seemed blessedly normal. He didn't have many moments like that any more.

You want more of them.

He rubbed his jaw with his knuckles. 'It's been a lovely afternoon, Chloe.'

'It has.' She laughed, the tinkling, magical sound filling the room. A room that hadn't known much joy since he'd moved in.

He wanted in on the joke. 'What's so funny?'

Her hair fell forward for a moment, masking her cheeks, and then she looked up, embarrassment dancing around her dimples. 'I guess I wasn't expecting us to have a fun time. I mean, who knew, right?'

'Who knew indeed?' His laughter joined hers as he thought about their inauspicious start a few weeks ago, but today they'd got along well and he appreciated her no-nonsense honesty. Unlike so many of his friends and colleagues, she didn't tiptoe around him, wondering what to say and making him feel edgy in the process. Chloe made him laugh and he needed that. He wanted it. He wanted more afternoons like today.

The only thing he didn't want was the rush of heat that came alive between them now and then, but neither did she, so where did that leave them?

Friends.

He saw the allure of that—uncomplicated time spent together. Win-win for both of them. A declaration of friendship would also draw a line in the sand, leaving no room for ambiguity. That alone would douse the fire that burned between them and totally reset things. With friendship on the table, it would give them clear and precise instructions on how to move forward with no misunderstandings. He raised his glass. 'To friendship.'

As she rolled her shoulders back, her hair brushed her jaw, sliding across her tilted chin. Clear eyes met his and, with a faint smile playing on the bow of her top lip, she raised her glass and tapped it gently against his. 'To friendship. Pure and simple.'

Heat licked his blood.

There's nothing simple about it.

He drained his glass in one big gulp.

'And here's the miracle-worker now,' Kate said as Chloe arrived on the ward for her afternoon shift.

Chloe glanced behind her, looking around for the person they were obviously talking to, but she found no one. She immediately checked her watch. 'I'm not late, am I?'

'You're fine,' Keri said, shaking her head indulgently. 'Kate's being silly and celebrating.'

'Oh, why? What's happened?'

Kate exchanged a knowing look with Keri before saying, 'I've just done an entire ward round with Luke Stanley.'

'Poor you.' The automatic response—the one used by every nurse on the ward in relation to Luke Stanley—tripped off her tongue.

That's not strictly fair any more.

She ignored her censuring inner voice as Kate continued.

'He was polite, well mannered, and he only had *one* complaint, and that was perfectly reasonable.'

Chloe smiled. 'That *is* worth celebrating.'

Keri nodded. 'And there's more. While you've been swanning about on your days off, we've had four...' she held up her left hand with her thumb crossing her palm '...that's *four* days of Luke being easier to work with. Even Richard's smiling again without the aid of chocolate.'

'That's great news,' Chloe said, picking up the roster and starting to assign nurses to patients.

She hadn't seen Luke since Saturday night when she'd thanked him and left his house after eating way too much of the delicious satay beef and chicken and even more of the spicy peanut sauce. Luke, who'd complained of being starving, hadn't ended up eating much at all and she'd noticed he'd taken some ginger for an upset stomach. Soon after that she'd left because he'd been looking exhausted but had been too polite to mention his weariness.

On Monday, she'd messaged him a photo of Amber with Chester on the beach. The puppy's coat had shimmered golden against Amber's inky curls, but it was the smile of delight on the little girl's face that had made Chloe's heart yearn and laugh. His reply text had thanked her for the photo and for helping him out on Saturday. At least, that was what she thought it meant because *Gear photon rhnkas agoa for saris eat* didn't make a lot of sense. It was either auto-correct gone mad or Amber had got to his phone and pressed random buttons.

Chloe was truly pleased that last Saturday seemed to have been a turning point for Luke. Perhaps admitting that he was finding it tough juggling work and home had relaxed him enough so that he wasn't being as difficult or demanding at work.

'And we owe it all to you,' said Kate.

Her head snapped up as a spark of adrenaline zipped around her, putting every part of her on alert. 'I don't understand.'

'No need to be coy with us, Chloe. We know.'

A sinking feeling weighted down her stomach. 'Know what?'

'That you spent time on the beach with your dog, Luke and his little girl.'

How was it that the Gold Coast, with its population of almost half a million, could mimic a small town?

Because you used the beach close to where many of the hospital staff live, stupid.

'I did.' Chloe concentrated on assigning the afternoon staff, matching their skills with the patients' needs and definitely not offering Keri any more information about last Saturday. She'd learned a long time ago that it was best to wait and find out what people actually knew before volunteering more.

'And...?' Keri's tone was full of interest.

'Chester was a big hit with Amber. I guess because he's close to her size,' Chloe said, as she calculated exactly how she was going to juggle things to cover the dinner break.

'I think Chloe was a big hit with Luke.' Kate nudged her gently as she prepared to do the dangerous drug handover count.

'I doubt that very much.' Chloe flinched at the inference that she and Luke were more than just friends. She hated it that she still felt sad whenever she thought about his *let's be friends* declaration because it should have thrilled her. She should have high-fived the man because wasn't she all about keeping her life simple? Not doing the relationship thing with any guy, let alone a grieving widower with a child?

'All I'm saying is that the man's been a different doctor since Monday morning.' Kate's brows rose knowingly. 'You do the maths.'

Chloe decided to play it straight because she didn't want to draw any more attention to herself. 'I just happened to be around when he needed a hand with Amber. Remember, his wife hasn't been dead all that long.'

Kate shrugged. 'It's been over a year and he won't grieve for ever.'

The memory of the baby girl who'd been ripped from her all those years ago dumped over her again. Her jaw tightened, making it hard to speak. 'There's no time limit on grief.'

'He's a man with a child, Clo,' Kate said matter-of-factly, as if her words explained everything.

Chloe frowned as a rising sense of outrage started to simmer. She didn't really understand why she was feeling like this but everything told her to keep it under control.

Her mouth didn't listen. 'Exactly what is *that* supposed to mean?'

'It means he'll eventually want a mother for his child,' Keri said, giving Chloe's shoulder a friendly squeeze. 'I'll let you in on a secret. Often the best relationships are the result of one person being in the right place at the right time.'

A flare of fury burned under her ribs and she shrugged Keri's hand away. 'What are you both saying? That I'm waiting in the wings for him to notice me? Look, I helped him out *once*. End of story. Do *not* read more into this than there is and don't go creating a future that's never going to happen.'

Her heart hammered hard against her ribs with an intensity that stunned her. She told herself to stay calm, but as her hands slapped her hips she knew calmness had fled long ago. 'Just because Luke Stanley has a Y chromosome doesn't mean he's automatically looking for a mother for his child. He's still very much in love with Anna. But all that aside—' her voice rose dangerously high '—when have I ever said I wanted to be a mother?'

Keri's eyes widened and she took a step back with her hands held high. 'Whoa, Chloe.'

She wanted to drop her head in her hands and tear at her hair but that would only make things worse. Oh, God, why had she overreacted? She never did that. She was the epitome of calmness and good cheer—a public persona she'd worked really hard at so she could avoid exposing herself in situations like this.

Shame you couldn't do it today.

She may as well have put a huge flashing sign over her head advertising the fact she was single for more reasons than just not having met the right guy. Oh, why had she even mentioned motherhood to two women who were career mothers?

'Sorry, Chloe,' Kate said, her face stricken. 'We thought you'd be fine with some teasing.'

She racked her brain for a reply—one that could give a reasonable excuse for her outburst and keep these two insightful women far, far away from the truth. Her brain bounced from option to option. The tried and true default excuse of being tired wasn't going to work this time because she'd just had four days off.

For some reason, the memory of the flare of desire in Luke's eyes last Saturday, followed by his horrified expression, rose in her mind.

To friendship. He'd retreated from desire because he still loved his wife, and there was her excuse.

She swallowed and wrung her hands. 'I'm sorry, I overreacted, it's just if you'd seen his face when he talked about Anna…' She mustered a wry smile, letting the silence work for her before saying, 'So shall we do the dangerous drug count?'

Kate and Keri nodded, allowing her deliberate change of topic to go through without hindrance. Only Chloe knew both of them too well to know that this was unlikely to be the end of it. They'd try again, but forewarned was forearmed and next time she'd be ready.

CHAPTER SIX

'CHLOE, HAVE YOU got any ibuprofen?'

Luke stood at the nurses' station, looking like death warmed up. His presence on the ward was unexpected, given he'd completed his rounds earlier with Kate. It was the first time she'd seen him since Saturday and back then he hadn't looked one hundred per cent either.

'Have you got a temperature?' Her hand automatically shot to his forehead, her palm registering the heat of his skin. It wasn't overly warm but it still made her palm tingle and she stifled the delicious shiver that threatened to shoot straight to the apex of her thighs and make her sigh.

His eyes darkened to moss green at the familiarity of her touch and waves of tension beat at her palm.

What are you doing?

She quickly jerked her arm away and embarrassment swept through her, chasing out her craving for him and leaving only excruciating awkwardness. How could she have touched him like that? Like she had the right to be in his personal space when she had no right at all, especially after his explicit statement about being friends.

Friends, Chloe. Friends. Get it right. 'I'm sorry. I shouldn't have done that, I…' The tight look on his face stole her words. *Oh, hell, shoot me now.*

He'd fixed his gaze on the wall behind her and his lips, which had pressed into a straight line, now softened slightly. 'There's no need to be sorry. You're a nurse and it's an instinctive action.' He moved his head with a jerk, as if he was making himself look at her. 'I don't have a fever. I just have a normal headache, which isn't budging.'

She thought about his upset stomach from a few days ago. 'Headaches and nausea. Sounds like you're prodromal and fighting a virus.'

He rubbed his eyes and shook his head. 'No. It's probably just allergies. I'll swing by the pharmacy and get some nasal spray but meanwhile

I'd appreciate some paracetamol or ibuprofen to nuke the headache so I can get through the out-patients' hand clinic.'

'Sounds like you've got a busy afternoon.' She passed him the analgesia and poured a glass of water from the filtered-water dispenser.

'Busy is good.' He quickly tossed back the tablets and chased them down with the chilled water.

'True.' Her eyes strayed to his Adam's apple, which rose and fell as he swallowed—a delectable bulge that delineated the strength of his neck.

Heady need returned, storming through her and making her swallow. She dropped her gaze fast, pulling her chin down and hiding behind a curtain of hair that fell forward, thankfully covering the flush she could feel burning her cheeks. Why, oh, why did he have to be such a perfect specimen of a man? It should be illegal for a man to have such thick, dark lashes—lashes that caressed his cheeks when he blinked and made her think of butterfly kisses.

He threw the disposable cup across the space towards the bin. When it fell short and landed on the floor, he looked baffled. 'Has someone moved the bin?'

She laughed at his incredulity. 'No. Accept that you missed.'

'I never miss,' he said sharply, the word slicing through the air and reviving memories of the oft-intolerant surgeon he'd been up until a few days ago. 'I've been tossing things into that bin for three years.'

Having lived with her brother for many years, she knew the oddest things upset men, and obviously this uncharacteristic lack of co-ordination was an affront to Luke's ego. 'Like I said, perhaps you're fighting a virus and it's putting you off your game. Try and get to bed early tonight.'

Oh, my God, shut up! You are not his mother.

His thunderous expression cleared as his wide and generous mouth pulled up into a grin, sending sexy creases into his jet stubble. He gave her a mock salute. 'Yes, Ms Kefes, I promise to take care of myself.'

She wanted the floor to open up and swallow her. *Friendship pure and simple,* her brain taunted her.

If every meeting was going to be like this one—lurching from lust-fuelled desire to attempting to be a dispassionate work colleague while trying to find the right level of friendship—she was probably going to have to step back completely and return to the surgeon and nurse relationship they'd had before.

Luke spun on his heel, wondering where the camaraderie he and Chloe had finally found on Saturday had gone. She seemed tense and was in full-on nurse mode, except when she'd pressed her hand against his forehead it hadn't felt like a clinical touch at all. He'd wanted to cover her hand with his own, slide it gently down his face to his lips, kiss her palm and then trace her life-line with his tongue.

Thank God, guilt had slewed through him, whipping him hard and reminding him of *all* the reasons why he couldn't do that—the very least of them being because they were standing in a public ward in their workplace.

Anna would be here today if it wasn't for you. The least you can do is respect her memory.

I am, damn it. Chloe and I are just friends.

The thought reminded him of something and he turned back towards Chloe. 'Ah, Chloe, I've been meaning to thank you for sending me that photo of Amber on the beach. Sorry I didn't get back to you sooner.' He shrugged, aiming for added casualness to mask how very non-casual he really felt. 'You know how it is.'

Her kaleidoscope eyes, with their flecks of green and brown, dazzled him with surprise. 'You already thanked me. You sent me a text.'

He tilted his head, trying to shake free the memory, but he got nothing. The recollection of her text arriving was crystal clear and he could easily picture her name appearing on his phone. The memory gave him the same buzz he'd experienced when it had arrived four days ago. Back then he'd wanted to reply straight away but he'd looked at Anna's photo and had made himself wait.

Unlike lust-fuelled lovers, who replied instantly, desperate for the next rush of a return text, platonic friends waited. They could only be friends. He had *not* sent the text.

'I think, Chloe, I'd have remembered if I'd done

that.' Sarcasm he couldn't stop oozed through the words.

Her chestnut brows drew down, setting off a tremor that rolled across her straight, slim shoulders, over and around her generous feminine curves until it reached her sensibly work-shoe-shod feet. Every single part of her screamed, *He's lost the plot.*

Her smile was muted. 'Granted, most of the text was gobbledygook and it didn't make a lot of sense.'

'Amber must have got to my phone,' he said, calling on a lie. Amber was not allowed anywhere near his phone because it was a work tool. No patient or colleague ringing with an urgent request should have to deal with a toddler.

As he heard Chloe's murmured acquiescence, his mind grappled with the continual and unnerving blankness about the text. It wasn't the first time he'd had blanks like this—the missing cheese, the chips in the fridge, his sister gently reminding him that he'd already phoned her earlier in the day to tell her he'd organised a plumber to fix their pool pump that had failed.

Plenty of single parents coped with a gruelling job and raising a child and they did it without losing their marbles. Why was he finding it so hard? Was it all down to grief?

Honestly, Luke, how do you manage complicated surgery when you can't even remember to buy milk on the way home?

Anna's voice, which had started to fade over the months, suddenly boomed loud and clear in his head. He instantly relaxed. All of his blanks were to do with home and family tasks—none of them pertained to work. Anna had run their domestic lives with precision and vigour, and he'd rarely had to do anything in that realm.

When he'd got back from France Steph had supported him but now, with her on holiday, he was doing everything, plus checking on her property and working full time. All of it was a steep learning curve. Everything would get easier—he just needed some practice.

A patient's buzzer rang, jolting him out of his thoughts. 'I'll let you get back to it.'

'Yes.' Her feet didn't move.

He got an intense feeling she wanted to say

something to him but instead of opening her mouth her teeth snagged the plumpness of her bottom lip.

His heart kicked up. *Leave now.* 'Have a good afternoon.'

His words came out tighter and harsher than he'd intended and seemed to jerk her out of deep thought.

'You too. Bye.'

She walked away from him, straight towards Room Three to attend to Mr Tran, whom he'd operated on earlier in the day to release a tight hand contracture.

He hauled his gaze from the sweet swing of her hips and strode towards the elevators that would take him to Outpatients and, thankfully, to back-to-back patient appointments that would keep him completely occupied for the next three hours. His mind would be full of his patients' problems and there'd be no time or room to think about anything else.

Not Anna. Not the fact he'd missed an easy shot at the bin, and definitely not about huge, hazel eyes in a smiling, round face that had held concern for him.

Concern that scared the hell out of him.

Chloe was working yet another afternoon shift. Thursdays on Ward Six were always frantic because it was one of two elective surgery operating days. Granted, any day could be busy because emergencies happened randomly, but the pace of the ward always picked up on Wednesday afternoons, starting with the paperwork and history taking connected with admitting a new patient. Twenty-four hours later the ward was in full swing and handovers were done at the end of the bed because no one could be spared off the floor.

Chloe had always thought the most sensible staffing roster would be if Keri and Kate split up the day between them so that the unit manager and her second-in-command covered sixteen of the busiest twenty-four hours between them. But ideas and real life didn't always collide. Keri took her daughter to mini-musicians class on Thursday afternoons and Kate's boys played basketball. It appeared that neither of these events could happen on different days, which meant on most Thursdays, just as the ward reached its zenith of activity, Keri and Kate departed, leaving Chloe in charge. Today was no exception and Chloe had moved puppy school to Fridays.

When she was in charge, she arrived thirty minutes earlier than her allotted start time so she could get a handle on the ward before her staff arrived. Today she was here even earlier, but instead of taking the lift up to Ward Six, she pressed the 'LG' button and got out at the operating theatre suite. Pulling on scrubs, shoe covers and a hair cover, she made her way to the viewing area outside Theatre Three.

The small gallery was almost full of medical students and interns but she spied a seat in the far corner at the front. No one had taken it as it involved eight people standing up to allow access. She had no qualms at all making them stand up because she refused to stand on her tippytoes at the back. She wanted a front-row seat to watch Luke performing this rather unusual operation.

The theatre was full of staff, including two operating teams along with two scout nurses. Richard, close to graduating as a plastic surgeon, was leading the team that was harvesting the toe and Luke was in charge of the attachment team, bringing tiny nerves and arteries together and repairing tendons so the toe could function as a thumb.

'Why isn't he using the big toe?' one of the medical students wondered out loud.

'Balance,' she replied, and all eyes turned to her, filled with surprise that a nurse had the answer.

They didn't know she'd spent a rapt hour yesterday listening to Luke telling her about how Ethan Popovic had lost a finger in a sheet-metal factory accident and how he was going to transplant one of his toes to his hand.

They also had no clue that she'd had the privilege of hearing him explain the specialised angiograms of the patient's left hand and right foot, which showed the blood and nerve supply to both areas. He'd pointed out how he'd mapped the transplant and he explained the need to structure the bone of the toe to fit its new function as a thumb.

Throughout the explanations he'd been the surgeon, she'd been the nurse and they'd spent a companionable time together. She'd been fascinated and enthralled, but mostly she'd been relaxed because talking about work with Luke was safe. Very safe. And she needed safe with him because anything else was murky, unclear and completely unsettling.

'The patient's only twenty-five,' she explained to the crowd, 'and he's into extreme sports. If he'd lost his big toe it would impact on his ability to return to rock climbing. This way he has a chance, but using the second toe actually makes the surgery more complicated.'

'Cool.' The student was impressed.

A screen in the room allowed for close-up views of the surgery but as this wasn't a specific teaching operation there were no microphones and the volume had been switched off. It was hard to read expressions on theatre staff as their faces were covered by masks, so Chloe used their body language to gauge the tone of the theatre and to see how everyone was faring at the five-hour mark of a possible seven-hour operation.

The scout and scrub nurses—the litmus test of tensions in the operating theatre—were doing their usual visual code and eyes were shining, which was a good sign. Richard had stepped back, his role in the surgery over, and his forehead was clear of any frown marks. Luke's shoulders were square but not overly tense, and his long, tapered fingers moved surely and easily, almost underplaying the difficulty of the delicate and minute work they were doing.

A sense of awe and wonder flowed through her at his talent. His skill was out and out amazing and a flash of something flared inside her. She realised she was proud of him. She wanted to turn around and say to those around her, *Be really impressed. You're seeing something truly special.* She smiled to herself. Maybe she was finally getting a hang of this friendship thing after all.

Luke glanced up from the surgical field for a moment, staring out towards the window, his eyes bright green behind wide, clear protective glasses. Leaving her arm close to her side, she flicked up her hand in a low wave—a private and supportive acknowledgment that she was there. There for him. As a friend.

She waited for the flash of recognition to spark in his eyes so she could imagine his endearing smile hidden behind his mask. Granted, he didn't smile a lot but when he did it lit up his face and she could glimpse the man he'd once been— happy and content.

His stare continued, only it was vacant and un-responsive. She tried not to give in to the chill of disappointment that settled like a lead brick in her belly.

He's concentrating, that's all.

She wanted to believe that but there was some-thing about his gaze that troubled her.

He did this when you were at his house. He swayed.

Oh, God. Her breath froze in her lungs, her hands tensed in her lap and she wanted to dive through the glass that separated them and grab him.

A second later Luke blinked, his eyes franti-cally flicking left and right, up and down, as if he was confirming where he was and what he was doing. He gave a curt nod to the scrub nurse, who immediately wiped his brow with a gauze swab, and then his fingers started moving again, returning to making minuscule stitches.

Chloe blew out the breath she'd been holding and glanced around. No one else seemed to have noticed the moment when time had stood still. There'd been no ripple of concern from the theatre staff either—no widened eyes, no frowns, and neither of the scout nurses had moved quickly, yet she was certain she hadn't imagined that empty look, as if Luke had vanished for a moment.

You're overthinking it.

You need to talk to him.

Her watch beeped, reminding her it was time to head up to the ward. Most of her didn't want to move but she had to make sure everything was ready for when their patient arrived back from Recovery. Apologising to the others, she sidled out, her legs brushing theirs, and made her way straight up to the ward.

'How's it going down there?' Keri asked the moment she arrived.

'Good, I think. The patient's probably ninety minutes away.'

Keri nodded. 'We've delayed Mrs Luciano's pre-med.'

'Luke's doing another operation today?' Chloe couldn't believe that he would do that on the back of such challenging surgery.

'He's got another two. They're quick and easy carpal tunnels but even so, you're going to be busy tonight.'

'Always am on Thursdays.' Chloe smiled.

'That's what I want to talk to you about. Kate's pregnant and—'

Pregnant. Chloe's blood seemed to whoosh to her feet as she tried not to let her own regrets and pain swamp her.

Keri laughed at her expression. 'I know. It's a huge surprise, especially as Phil had a vasectomy.'

Not just pregnant but unplanned too.

More than a decade may have passed since she'd been pregnant but loss and regret lingered, waiting to rush back in and remind her that she would never experience pregnancy again—planned or unplanned.

She forced the muscles of her face to pull her mouth into a smile. It was like moving concrete. 'Kate's pregnant? How great is that?'

'Well, it is now she's got her head around it,' Keri said prosaically. 'At first she was pretty cut up about it because they only wanted two and a third means a bigger car and extending the house.'

'I can see that,' Chloe said faintly, not believing her words for a moment. So many people took pregnancy for granted and it was only those who couldn't conceive who realised there was nothing ordinary or everyday about it at all.

'Anyway...' Keri got back on track '...I want you to apply to be second-in-charge when Kate's on maternity leave. You're an asset to the ward and you're doing the job a lot of the time anyway. You deserve to have the formal position, which will look good on your résumé, and I'm imagining that the extra money won't hurt either.'

'That's very true.' Chloe wanted to squeal and high-five, but she kept her excitement in check.

Keri smiled. 'It's an advertised position so you have to apply and jump through the hoops. However, I'll be giving you a glowing reference.'

'Thanks, Keri, I appreciate your faith in me.'

The unit nurse manager checked her watch. 'We'd better start handover or I'll be late for Tahlia's music.' She started walking down the corridor to the patient's room.

'Maddie phoned in sick so I've organised an agency nurse to cover her patients. Mr Morgan's IV needs resiting and as you've got the knack with his dodgy veins, we've waited for you. His dressing is now twice daily and you might need to pacify his wife because she's worried that...'

And we're on. Chloe started writing notes and strategising the shift, all other thoughts pushed firmly out of her mind.

The shift was ticking along nicely. The patients had been fed and many were being entertained by visitors, which gave the nurses a little hiatus from answering buzzers and left them free to get on with other jobs.

'Who's in charge?'

Chloe jumped as she recognised the furious strains of Luke's voice blasting into the air from further down the ward. 'Then go and find her. Please.' Luke's steely tone turned the pleasantry into a lethal weapon.

At the yell, the student nurse Chloe was supervising while she undertook Mr Morgan's dressing dropped the tweezers onto his belly, breaking the sterilization.

'Someone's not happy,' the jovial man said with typical Australian understatement.

'Apparently not.' Chloe wanted to rush out of the room and find out what on earth was going on but first she said, 'Emily, you need to de-glove, get new tweezers and glove up again. You're right to do that without me, aren't you?'

The student nodded, her eyes wide as the sound of Luke's fury slid under doors, boomed around curtains and filled every space.

'Good.' Chloe mustered her best professional voice, given the inexcusable yelling that was raging around them. 'Excuse me, Mr Morgan, I'll be back as soon as I can.'

'Take your time, love,' Mr Morgan said with a

wink. 'I thought it was only the neurosurgeons who were the volatile ones.'

She hurried out into the corridor to find the agency nurse, Jean, speed-walking towards her.

'Chloe, the plastic surgery consultant wants to talk to you. I don't know what the problem is but he's seriously cross.' Jean touched her arm. 'Do you want me to come with you?'

'Thanks, but I'll be fine.'

Jean didn't look convinced. 'Are you sure?'

She nodded, despite the thread of anxiety that was building inside her. She found Luke pacing back and forth outside the nurses' station. Anger beamed off him but underneath it all she saw shadows of exhaustion. She bit her lip. She'd never seen him this wound up before. What was going on with him?

'Luke,' she said firmly, 'I believe you wish to speak to me.'

He spun around—an unrecognisable six-foot-four-inch tower of fury—with eyes blazing and every tendon bulging. 'You bet I do. What the hell sort of a shoddy—?'

She held up her hand like a stop sign. 'Let's

go into the treatment room first, shall we?' She walked towards the room, giving him no other choice than to follow.

His long, firm strides quickly overtook her smaller ones. 'Fine,' he ground out of a mouth so taut it must have hurt to speak, 'but telling you in private won't change the fact you've stuffed up royally.'

His fury buffeted her and Chloe closed the door behind them, leaning against it for a brief moment to gather her reserves. She didn't recognise this Luke and she didn't like him. 'What's upset you so much that you've broken protocol by yelling on my ward?'

His arms flew out in front of him, gesticulating widely. 'I've broken protocol? Now, that's rich.'

'The problem, Luke?' she prompted quietly, trying to direct his anger to the cause and bypass the personal attack.

'The problem is...' his voice rose in derision '...that right now I'm supposed to be operating on Mrs Lewinski, but instead of fasting I've just walked into the ward to find her scarfing chocolates.'

Chloe felt herself frown. 'Are you sure?'

His black curls bounced with resentment. 'I'm not blind, Chloe. Of course I'm sure.'

She'd inadvertently confused him. 'Sorry, I meant are you sure Mrs L. is on the list? I don't recall seeing her name.'

His shoulders squared to right angles. 'Are you calling me a liar?'

She swallowed a sigh, wondering where the reasonable man whose company she'd enjoyed so much had gone. 'No,' she said, keeping her voice steady despite her hammering heart. 'I'm dealing with facts.'

She pulled the printed theatre list out of her pocket and scanned it. 'Her name's not here.'

'Let me look at that.' He jerked the paper out of her fingers so fast that a corner ripped.

'A "*please*" would have sufficed,' she muttered, fast losing patience with his rudeness.

Luke didn't respond. He was too busy staring wild-eyed and disbelievingly at the list. 'You've obviously got the wrong version.'

Pointing to the date and time at the bottom, she said, 'This was updated at three. I've taken every phone call since then and there haven't been any calls from you or Theatre, making changes.'

She rested her hand on his arm for a moment, thinking about how he'd stared at her through the glass but hadn't actually seen her. 'You've been so preoccupied with the Popovic case, perhaps you thought you'd told us to add Mrs L. to the list but in actual fact you forgot to make the call.'

He threw her hand off his arm with a jerk. 'Don't patronise me.'

'I'm not.' Her fraying patience snapped. 'I'm trying to find a reason why you're behaving so obnoxiously. You do realise that you are?'

Stormy seas didn't come close to matching the swirl of emotions in his eyes. 'I'm *trying* to do my job.'

'This isn't the way to do it.' She met his gaze and took the hit of his wrath. 'Everyone here tells me how understanding and accommodating you were before…' *Oh, God, why did I just go there?*

His eyes narrowed to taunting slits of green. 'Go on. Say it.'

As every part of him turned rigid, she realised that if she'd thought his body had been tight with tension before, she'd been way off the mark. He was strung so taut he might shatter. Sympathy diluted her infuriation with him. 'Luke, I didn't—'

'Yes, you did.' His gaze—like the sights of a loaded gun—pinned her to the wall. 'You wanted to say, before my wife died. Or, to be more precise, before I killed her.'

'Don't be ridiculous.' Her words shot out of her mouth as every part of her rejected what he'd said. She knew innately he was wrong. Oh, so very wrong. 'You didn't kill Anna.'

He shuddered and dragged his hands through his hair, curls tangling with his fingers like tropical vines. 'Oh, yes, I did. I drove my beautiful wife, the only woman I've ever loved, into the path of an oncoming car.'

His grief and guilt hit her like a tsunami, catching her up in its massive grasp and rolling her over and over before flinging her, winded, onto the shore. She didn't think—she just moved instinctively. Her hands cupped his cheeks and she tilted his head down, angling it so he couldn't look anywhere but at her.

Luke felt the warmth of her fingers on his face

and recognised the entreaty in her eyes but none of it was enough to change a damn thing. God, he'd just gone ballistic and been insufferable with Chloe, and accused everyone of doing the wrong thing when he'd been the one firmly at fault. How could he have been so adamant that he'd put Mrs Lewinski on the list when he'd never made the call?

You are seriously losing your mind.

What if you lose your cool with Amber? What if you tear into her like this?

The thought choked him and he dug his thumbs into his temples, trying to deaden the daily throb that had become a part of him. Anna had been dead for over a year but his life was still spiralling out of control, with grief firmly in the driver's seat. Driving him. He hated it and yet no matter what he tried, he lacked power over it. Six months ago Steph had suggested he see a grief counsellor and, desperate to do something, he'd gone. Once. He'd left angry when she'd told him that time would heal. Over a year had passed and time had done squat.

'Luke.' Chloe's voice implored in the unruffled

and reasonable tone he'd come to associate with her. 'Listen to me. Anna's death was an accident. A car accident.'

He shook his head but her hands held him so tightly it barely moved. 'It was an accident I caused. I drifted onto the wrong side of the road and the gendarmes said I must have fallen asleep at the wheel.'

Her hands moved to his shoulders. 'Do you think you did?'

She'd just asked the question that tormented him every single day. 'No. Yes. I don't know. I never had before.'

Intelligent eyes scanned his face. 'Were you exhausted at the time?'

He closed his eyes for a moment and when he opened them she was still waiting for his reply. 'No. That's the thing. I was working at Le Centre Léon-Bérard in Lyon, doing post-cancer reconstructive surgery. We'd been there a couple of months and I always had *mercredi*…' He corrected himself. 'Wednesday afternoons off. We used the time to visit somewhere new in the Lyon district and that day our neighbour had offered to mind Amber and insisted we dine at Le Petit Cochon. The accident happened on the way there.'

'What do you remember about it?'

He squinted, trying yet again to visualise the scene and to conjure up more information, but he saw the same image he always got. 'Anna was laughing at something I'd tried to say in mangled French. She spoke it so much better than I did.'

The dull throb behind his eyes intensified. 'The next thing I can remember is waking up to crushed metal, the scream of sirens and no clue where the hell I was.' He gripped her arms tightly as his throat threatened to close. 'I killed her, Chloe, and I can't remember a damn thing about it.'

He wanted to lean his forehead against hers, seek her comfort and warmth, but he didn't deserve any of it. He spun on his heel, moving fast, away from the touch of her hands and the sympathy in her eyes. The abrupt movement made the floor tilt and silver spots bounce in front of his eyes. Nausea clogged his throat and everything spun.

He grabbed at a metal dressing trolley, trying to steady himself, but it skated away from him. He tried again and heard the jarring clatter of metal hitting linoleum. The contents of his stomach burned his throat and then he gagged. Vomit filled his mouth and he hurled.

'Luke!'

Chloe's voice sounded shrill and faint. Darkness crept across his mind and he threw out his arms, trying to grab her. His knees jerked out from under him. Everything went black.

CHAPTER SEVEN

FOR A SPLIT second Chloe stared, horrified, as Luke writhed on the floor at her feet with his eyes rolled back, vomit and blood pouring from his mouth and his muscles jerking and spasming. He was fitting—a full-blown, tonic-clonic seizure.

Move! She slammed her palm onto the emergency buzzer located on the wall, grabbed a plastic oropharyngeal airway and fell to her knees, knowing she had to wait until the fit finished before she could slide it into his mouth. As his arms and legs flailed, she protected him from hitting any more equipment and injuring himself further.

Time slowed down to nothing, the fit seeming to go on and on for ever when in reality she knew it was less than two minutes.

Jean, the agency nurse, appeared, summoned by the emergency buzzer. 'Can I—? Oh, God.'

'Draw up diazepam, pass me that oxygen mask and then ring a code red.' Chloe tried to sound cool and controlled when every part of her screamed, *I am so scared for him.*

'I'm on it.'

Finally, Luke's jerking slowed and his pale face and blue lips started to flush pink.

'Luke.' She had no idea if he could hear her because, although he was breathing on his own, she was certain he was unconscious. 'I'm going to roll you onto your side.'

She went through the motions of preparing him for the recovery position. Starting on his right side, she placed his right arm at right angles to his body with the palm of his hand facing up and then she put his left hand onto his chest, palm down. Lifting the knee of his top leg, she bent his leg so his knee pointed at her and then she tugged. His body moved slowly onto his side.

She heard Jean hang up the phone after calling the code red. 'Luke, I'm suctioning your mouth.' She deftly moved the sucker around his mouth, and after checking his throat was clear she finally slid the plastic airway into his mouth. 'Now I'm going to put an oxygen mask on your face, okay?'

His beautiful green eyes fluttered open for a moment, their gaze unfocused and glazed, before closing again. His inky lashes brushed his cheeks.

Chloe bit her lip and stroked his forehead. *What's going on inside that intelligent brain, Luke?*

She didn't want to think about the thousand possibilities—none of them good—so instead she fitted the green elastic of the oxygen mask over the back of his head and tried to make the mask as comfortable as possible. Jean passed her a pillow she'd grabbed off the trolley and Chloe put it under his head.

The doors to the treatment door were flung open with a thud and the emergency response team rushed in. 'What have we got?' the ICU registrar asked.

Still on the floor, Chloe turned to face them. 'Luke Stanley. Postictal.'

The shocked expletive that fell from the registrar's mouth matched the stunned expressions on the rest of the team's faces. A fitting patient was never good, but it was always worse when it was one of Gold Coast City Hospital's own.

'I've given him oxygen and I'm about to put in an IV,' Chloe said, needing to focus on the clinical stuff because her mind didn't want to go anywhere near the fear that was tearing up and down her veins. Fear for Luke. Fear for Amber. Fear for herself. 'Then I'm accompanying him to MRI.'

Not one of them disagreed.

'Chloe?' Luke asked groggily, his eyes struggling to focus.

He knew he was lying down and all he could see were fuzzy silver bars, but his nostrils detected the fresh, fruity scent that was synonymous with Chloe. He tried to raise his head but pain ricocheted through him, making him gasp.

'I'm right here, Luke.' She squeezed his hand. 'Don't try to move. Do you know where you are?'

Banks of bright white lights made his head ache and a stinging sensation burned the back of his left hand. He closed his eyes, trying to make sense of it. The last thing he remembered was being in surgery. 'I'm at work.'

'You're in the radiography department.'

He heard her matter-of-fact tone but the words sounded like jabberwocky and skated across his mind, not sticking. Nothing made sense, especially not this foggy feeling. His free hand touched his leg. *Skin.* Where the hell were his scrubs? What was going on? His fingers found the edges of a hospital gown.

What the—?

Fear ripped through him, halting all the questions with a primal need to protect his child. He struggled to sit up. 'Amber. Where's Amber?' Searing pain dropped his head back to the pillow. 'Amber. Daycare. I need to pick her up.'

'Luke, you're about to have an MRI,' Chloe said softly. 'I've spoken to the daycare centre and if I have your permission, I can collect Amber for you.'

She'll be safe with Chloe. Relief flowed around the edges of confusion about an MRI. 'You have it.'

'I just need you to say that to the director.'

She held a phone to his ear and he heard the director's voice asking him if Amber could be released to Chloe Kefes. His mouth tasted like the bottom of a birdcage and his tongue felt thick and unwieldy but he managed to say, 'Yes.' A moment later the touch of the phone left his ear.

'Luke, it's Ken Mendaz,' a gravelly voice said.

He felt a broad hand touch his ankle as he recognised and decoded the broad accent of Gold Coast City's neurosurgeon. 'Why are you in Theatre with me, Ken?'

'We're in Radiography, Luke. Remember? You're going to have an MRI.'

MRI? Did he remember? Everything seemed to jumble together into a tangled mess he couldn't unravel. God, why did his brain feel like sludge? The only clear thought he had was that Amber was with Chloe. *No, going to be with Chloe.* He didn't know why but it felt right.

Male voices he didn't recognise told him to roll over and then he felt himself being lifted and lowered onto the machine's bed. As it started to move he called out frantically, 'Chloe.'

'Yes, Luke?'

'Amber needs her bunny.'

'It's all going to be fine, Luke. It's all going to be fine.'

Why did Chloe sound like she was going to cry? It was the last clear thought he had before the blackness crept back in.

'Hey, bro', how's it going? You'll never guess—'

'I'm not Luke. I'm Chloe Kefes. Is this Stephanie Markham?'

Chloe pressed Luke's phone up against her left ear while holding Amber on her hip with her right arm. The little girl had finally fallen asleep after fretting for over an hour and sobbing, 'Daddy, Daddy, Daddy.' Chloe had wanted to sob with her.

'Yes, this is Steph.' The voice was friendly but firm. 'Why are you using Luke's phone?'

'I work with your brother and I'm afraid he's not very well.' Chloe crossed her fingers. 'Are you able to get back to the Gold Coast tonight?'

'Oh, God. What's happened?'

Chloe closed her eyes at the dread in Luke's sister's voice. There was no easy way to break this news. 'Luke's being operated on right now for a…' she grabbed a steadying breath '…brain tumour.'

A cry of despair howled down the line and then she heard a deeper male voice in the background saying, 'Honey, what's wrong?'

That was followed by a fainter, 'It's Luke.'

'Is he going to be all right?' Steph's tremulous question hung in the air.

I don't know. I wish I did. The picture of Luke on the operating table with the back of his head devoid of curls and shaved clean, with a central line in his chest and an endotracheal tube in his mouth, slugged her. The tear on her heart, which had been lengthening all evening, ripped a little bit more.

'We'll know more when he's out of the operating theatre and after the pathology comes back,' Chloe said, trying to sound professional and together. 'I'm ringing you because you're listed as Luke's next of kin and Amber needs her family. I'm caring for her at the moment but how soon can you arrive?'

Silence vibrated up and down the line.

Slight panic skidded through her. 'Stephanie?'

'Oh, Chloe,' she wailed. 'We're stranded in Arkaroola. It's been raining here and further north for over a week. All the creeks are flooded, the roads are washed away and...ten days...' the line hissed and spat, starting to break up '...more...get out.'

Her head pounded with the enormity of Luke's sister's news and desperation made her say, 'What about a plane? A helicopter?' *Anything.*

'Sorry...ranger...police...text...reception... Amber...love.'

The line went dead.

Chloe stared at the phone. It was the twenty-first century but the tyranny of distance in the outback was still as real today as it had been a hundred years ago. Luke's sister, his only next of kin, wasn't able to get home to care for him. Luke was alone.

Amber stirred against her shoulder—a defence-less little girl already without a mother, and right now her father was fighting for his life.

She dropped her head gently onto Amber's soft curls, breathing in the sweet smell of baby soap, feeling the weight of the child in her arms and the soft thump of her heart against her chest. Chloe's heart quivered. Amber was a child full of life—not a memory of a life not lived—and she needed care and protection. *My protection.*

'Oh, sweetie, life's so not fair,' Chloe murmured into her hair, uncertain if she'd spoken the words for Amber's benefit or her own.

'Chloe. Wake up.'

She felt a hand on her shoulder and her eyes flew open to see black leather. *Where am I?*

It all came flooding back. She was curled up around Amber, both of them sleeping on a couch in the ICU staff room, tucked up under theatre towels. She sat up and immediately made sure Amber was still covered.

Sarah Watson, an ICU nurse, held out a mug of soup towards her. 'Here.'

'Thanks.' She accepted the proffered drink. 'What time is it?'

'Three.'

Three a.m. Nine hours since Luke had fitted in front of her. It seemed like a lifetime.

'Luke's awake but groggy,' Sarah said. 'I'll stay here with Amber while you go see him and then you must take her home. Both of you need a decent sleep.'

'Thanks.' Chloe stood slowly and automatically smoothed down her hair, which had fallen free of its tie hours ago. She was glad there wasn't a mirror about because she didn't even want to think what she looked like after sleeping rough in her uniform.

She made her way to the cubicle where Luke lay, his black hair the only colour about him. The machines of ICU surrounded him, somehow managing to dwarf a tall and vital man.

Pain shot through her. He looked so vulnerable.

She caught his right hand in hers and whispered, 'Luke.'

His eyes fluttered open and he smiled a goofy smile. 'Hey, babe,' he said softly. 'You came back.'

Her heart cramped and she stifled a cry. Something about his tone and expression told her unequivocally that he thought she was someone else. *He thinks you're Anna.*

A twinge twisted in her gut and she didn't know why it bothered her so much. 'I'm Chloe, Luke.'

The light from his eyes faded as his jaw jerked and then he closed his eyes. When he opened them, his focus was clear and penetrating. 'How's Amber?'

'Fast asleep. How are you doing?'

One side of his mouth twitched upwards. 'No so bad for a guy who's just had his head opened like a sardine can.'

She stroked her thumb across the back of his hand. 'You scared the hell out of us.'

He squeezed her hand. 'Sorry.'

'What do you remember?'

'Not that much. Ken told me it was a meningioma.'

She nodded. 'A benign brain tumour, thank God, but how something that causes so much havoc can be called benign is beyond me.'

'Slow growing,' he said succinctly. 'Cancer's faster.'

'So slow growing that the symptoms are insidious and only make sense in hindsight.' She took the moment to explain. 'Like chips in the fridge.'

He rubbed his jaw slowly as a light dawned in his eyes. 'And forgotten text messages.'

'Yes, and blacking out for short moments. Ken said, depending on what the tumour was pushing on at any given time, you could have had symptoms on and off for two years.' She took a leap of faith, needing to say the words and hoping he would truly hear them. 'As a friend, I have to tell you something important.'

He studied her face, his gaze holding steady. 'What's that?'

Say it. 'You didn't fall asleep at the wheel in France, Luke. It would have been a blackout. I'm sorry Anna's dead, but you don't hold any culpability. You had no control over this tumour. No one knew it was there. The car crash was truly an accident.'

She's right. Luke's sluggish mind had a moment of clarity and he closed his eyes, feeling Chloe's fingers tighten on his own. He let her genuine empathy seep into him. For months and months he'd whipped himself for falling asleep at the wheel, aghast at what he'd done and wondering how he'd allowed it to happen. The insoluble puzzle had its answer. He had his answer.

It won't bring my darling Anna back.

He knew that. But at the same time it seemed like a weight had lifted from his soul. 'I want to go home.'

Chloe's laugh held a hint of hysteria. 'Give it a week, Luke. There are things to organise, and your sister's stuck—'

'Two days.' He squeezed her hand and then, feeling the cloying pull of the drugs stealing his concentration, he let himself drift back into a peaceful sleep.

'We're home!' Chloe called out rather unnecessarily, given that Amber and Chester were already running through the house, squealing and barking and looking for Luke.

She dumped the shopping bags on the retro green Laminex table she was certain must have come with the cottage rather than Luke seeking it out at a market. Unzipping the blue cooler bag, she quickly threw all the cold things into the fridge. It was a normal domestic routine that took place in houses all around the country with men and women alike—one parent having taken the child out to give the other adult some breathing space. Only in this household nothing was normal. She wasn't the parent, Luke wasn't the partner and this wasn't even her home.

It has times when it feels like it.

Don't go there. Neither of us wants it and it's never going to happen.

'Hey.' Luke appeared in the kitchen with Amber on his shoulders and Chester bouncing next to him. Amber's hands ran back and forth over Luke's head, fascinated with the touch and feel of his now healed suture line and his hair.

Chloe still got a jolt of surprise whenever she saw his haircut—a number three he'd insisted she give him the day he'd got home from the hospital. Under the onslaught of the fast-moving clippers, his curls had fallen to the floor and she'd worried he'd regret their loss.

She'd been wrong. Instead of the short style making him look like a thug, it made his eyes a more arresting green and the rest of him leaner and more gorgeous than ever.

'Hey, yourself,' she said, her eyes taking her fill of him.

Snap out of it. Be the nurse. 'Did you sleep?'

He smiled as he lifted a squirming Amber off his shoulders and set her down at her little blue table. 'Yes, Nurse Kefes. I'm a good patient and I've had my afternoon nap, but I didn't sleep as long. I'm taking it as a good sign that I'm improving.'

He opened a tub of playdough for Amber and set her up with a muffin set and a sausage maker, before turning back to Chloe. 'I hear the park was a big success.'

'Ducks, Daddy,' Amber said excitedly. 'Bread. Feed ducks.'

'You did, sweetie.' Chloe laughed, remembering how amazing it had been to watch the little girl go from being tentative and clinging tightly to her legs to enthusiastically flinging bread at the quacking chestnut teals. Every day she felt a tiny bit of her heart leave her, stolen by the antics of Amber, especially when the little girl wrapped her pudgy arms around her neck and snuggled in close.

'I don't think she's hungry, though, because she ate more bread than she gave to the ducks.' A flicker of inadequacy churned her stomach and she frowned. 'I must remember to always take some food with me.'

'Chloe,' Luke said with mild reproof, 'you're doing an amazing job. I've had almost two years to learn all that stuff and you've been thrown in at the deep end. We can't thank you enough.' He leaned in and casually brushed his lips ever so briefly across her cheek before quickly pulling out a kitchen chair.

'Sit, Chloe.' His tone was so matter-of-fact he could have been calling Chester to heel. 'I'll rustle up a Vegemite sandwich for Amber and a coffee for you.'

'Thanks,' she said faintly, almost falling onto the chair. A blast of conflicting emotions rocked through her, stealing the strength from her legs. Again.

The kiss—no, it hadn't been a kiss, she told herself sternly. It had been an appreciative peck, a chaste touch.

It was something she could totally imagine him

giving his sister or a maiden aunt and it aptly summed up the surreal situation in which she was currently living. Every moment of every day she was straddling the line between being a caregiver and a platonic friend to a man who made her blood run hot and filled her dreams. Dreams that woke her panting, tingling and tangled up in her sheets.

All of it was utterly, mentally exhausting. All of it was dangerous to her long-fought-for safe and relationship-free life.

Two weeks had passed since Luke's surgery. His skin staples had been removed from his scalp and the only residual effects he'd experienced from having a benign tumour cut out of his brain were weariness and some minor co-ordination issues that were improving every day.

His moments of confusion in the first few days were now non-existent and recently there'd been times, when she was so tired from running around after Amber and caring for Luke, that he'd thought faster and more cogently than her.

'Steph called while you were out,' Luke said, over the hissing sound of steam through milk.

Luke's sister tried to phone every day for an update because she and her family were still stuck in the outback because of impassable roads. Although Chloe was yet to meet Steph, she'd initially spoken to her daily for the first week and she really liked the practical, no-nonsense woman. Just recently Luke had taken all the calls.

'How is she?' she asked, glad to have a topic of conversation that shut out the cacophony of thoughts that came under the banner of *way too complicated.*

'Frustrated.' He set a coffee down in front of her, complete with latte art of a fern, similar to the ones growing in the shady secret garden.

She adored spending time in Luke's garden and at some point every day she and Amber would go there and play with the water play set. Initially, Chloe had thought Amber would play on her own but she didn't seem keen to do so. After consulting some normal childhood development books, Chloe realised her expectations were far too high. Now she joined in playing tea parties and pouring water through the water wheel to make the boats sail.

Very occasionally Amber would get so involved in her play or be so engrossed with Chester that Chloe could actually take ten minutes of uninterrupted, blissful reading time.

Luke slid into the seat across from her, his expression serious. 'We all assumed Steph would be back by now and I feel that Amber and I are imposing on you.'

'Don't be silly,' she blurted out, rushing to reassure him despite the cautious voice in her head that said, *The longer this goes on the tougher it's going to be to leave.* 'What are friends for if not to help out?'

He frowned. 'Chloe, you've taken precious annual leave to work harder than you do at the hospital. I know how much work toddlers can be.'

She did too and she'd learned fast. 'Yes, but Amber's gorgeous and a joy to mind unless she's overtired. Not unlike someone a bit bigger than her,' she teased with a wink.

'Are you referring to a grumpy plastic surgeon?' His eyes sparkled and he gave her an impish grin.

The familiar swirl of attraction that she both

loved and loathed spun through her as it did every single time he smiled at her. She sobered. 'You're hardly grumpy any more. Having a tumour in your head can't have been easy.'

'So it appears.'

He got a far-away look in his eyes and she tried not to panic. He hadn't fitted since before the surgery and this look wasn't a blackout. She'd come to call it his *Anna look*. He did it occasionally when he was thinking about his wife.

He pulled back to the present. 'I feel more like myself than I have in a very long time.'

'I've noticed the difference.'

His gazed fixed on her so intently it was as if they were the only two people in the world. Her mouth dried and she wanted to dive into those pools of liquid green.

'I'm glad,' he said softly. 'I didn't like being that person.'

His words wove around her, charging the air between them and pulling them together. Her head tilted forward as if tugged by an invisible thread, and so did his. She could feel the warmth of his breath on her face, smell a hint of mint, see the flare of his nostrils and the sheen of sweat on his top lip.

Kiss him.

This time she didn't pause to argue. Instead, for the first time in two years she let her body take over. Her forehead tilted until it rested gently on his. Her eyes fluttered closed as her lips opened, ready to touch his lips.

Coolness streaked across her forehead, telling her he'd pulled back. Her eyes shot open and she saw him sitting ramrod straight in his chair with his fingers tightly interlaced and knuckles gleaming white.

'How's the coffee?' he asked, looking everywhere but at her.

Fighting the shock of disappointment that he'd moved away from her, she struggled for equilibrium. She slowly stirred her coffee, watching the beautiful fern pattern bleed away to a mess of brown and white. A mess that perfectly reflected her life.

Stupid, stupid, stupid, Chloe.

Apart from Nick, there wasn't a man out there

who cared much about her and she needed to remind herself of that. Right now.

She raised her chin, determined to look at him—to act as if she hadn't almost kissed him. Somehow, against a tight throat, she managed to croak out, 'It's a bit bitter.' *Or is that just me?*

She batted the thought away. 'Is this the new blend you asked me to pick up from the deli?'

'Yes.' He flicked open a magazine until he came to a page with a picture of a shiny machine that wouldn't look out of place in the space programme. 'I think I need a new coffee machine. What do you think of this one?'

She saw the five-digit figure and choked. 'That's six months' rent.'

Something close to guilt crossed his face. 'Talking of rent, can I pay yours while you're here? It's the least I can do with how much help you've been.'

That would be wonderful, thank you. But accepting his offer would only cause her more grief. She had to hold some part of herself back from Luke to survive. 'That's very kind of you, Luke, but it's all good. I've been taking care of myself for a very long time now and I've got it sorted.'

Deep creases furrowed his brow and he gave her a long enquiring look filled with concern.

A flutter of panic eddied in her gut that he was about to ask her why.

'Story, Daddy?' Amber appeared with her favourite book about a train and climbed up onto her father's knee.

Thank you, sweetie.

Luke pressed a kiss into Amber's hair. 'Sure thing.'

Two dark heads pored over the illustrations in the story, with Amber calling out, *'Toot-toot.'*

And Luke would reply, *'Off we go,'* in his deep, melodious voice. Both of them were so engrossed in the story it was like they were the only people in the room.

Chloe's heart lurched unexpectedly in her chest and she rose quickly, clearing the table and stowing the coffee mugs in the dishwasher. It was a timely reminder that Luke and Amber were a self-contained unit and she couldn't allow herself to think for a single moment that she belonged in that tableau.

CHAPTER EIGHT

CALLIE STARED AT the baby in front of her. He'd just been admitted and she'd finished examining him but was pulling blanks on his diagnosis. She liked to have some clues before ordering rafts of tests but today she was struggling.

'That's a really big frown for a pretty face, Dr Richards.'

A rush of heat stormed through her and she didn't need to look up to know exactly who was standing next to her. The man was sex on a stick and oozed charisma. As much as Callie had tried to tune out the hospital gossip, it was impossible because every second nurse and every third intern, irrespective of his or her gender, was trying to date the man.

Be cool, be calm, be detached, and at all costs be witty. 'Ah, the ever-charming Dr Coleman.' *That's not witty.* 'How are things?'

He smiled his easy smile—the one that lit up his face and lit up Callie. 'Things are good,' he said in his sexy American drawl. 'Better than you, I think.' He inclined his head towards the baby. 'Problems?'

'Yes.' She met his gaze and beyond the ever-present charm she detected professional concern for her little patient and a genuine interest.

Run the symptoms past him. He might be able to help.

Talking to Cade about the baby would also help her in her campaign of thinking of him only in terms of a fellow doctor—her current campaign to maintain precious distance. 'Would you mind talking through his history with me, please? I'm missing something.'

'Happy to.' He tilted his head, all professional attention. 'Shoot.'

Years of well-honed skills came to the fore. 'Baby Nicols, born at term and abandoned. Mother unknown. He's been in foster-care for four weeks but is irritable and failing to gain weight.'

'Drug screen results at birth?' Cade asked, as his high forehead creased in concentration.

'Not done.'

His brown brows rose sharply and if he'd wanted to blurt out, *'That would never happen in the States,'* he managed to stifle it.

Callie couldn't get all parochial or take offence at his expression because she'd been horrified herself when she'd found out the tests hadn't been carried out. 'I know it's supposed to be standard procedure when the patient's history isn't known, but the baby was born in the outback and examined in a tiny clinic. He appeared healthy at birth and, given the lack of medical infrastructure, everything stopped at a routine exam, despite the fact that he's not the most attractive baby on the planet—'

'Oh, I don't know.' Cade smiled his hypnotic smile. 'I've seen stranger-looking kids, that's for sure. So how's he ended up here on the glittering Gold Coast?' He stroked his finger along the baby's forehead.

Callie stared at the action, trying to align the

inveterate playboy with a man who was so gentle and caring with children.

'Callie?'

She quivered at the way his accent rolled over her name and was immediately horrified that her body had done that, let alone the fact she'd allowed her thoughts to be sidetracked. 'Um, the foster-mother's visiting her sister. She says today he won't feed at all and she's given him saline drops to try and clear his snuffly nose.'

Cade unlooped his stethoscope from around his neck and listened to the baby's heart rate. 'Slightly elevated, but that fits the story of baby with a cold.'

'That's what I thought but that doesn't account for the substantial weight loss. On the chart, he falls firmly into the failure-to-thrive category. His low weight gain isn't due to this cold.'

Callie reached over and undid the baby's nappy. 'This rash could be nappy rash except…' She picked up the baby's feet.

Cade blinked and moved in for a closer look. His cologne floated around Callie and she moved sideways so as not to breathe it in, knowing it would undermine her best intentions of staying detached.

He clicked on his penlight. 'I can see tiny blisters. Are they anywhere else?'

She nodded. 'Yes, on his hands and around his mouth too. With that pattern, the logical thought is *Candida* but it doesn't look anything like it.'

Cade scratched his head. 'So let's recap. Failure to thrive, irritable, the sniffles and a rash. All vague symptoms and could be due to a thousand things. Are you waiting on blood tests?'

'I was about to do them.'

He cupped the baby's cheek and using his torch examined the nose. 'Did the foster-mom say if the nasal discharge had ever been thick mucus?'

She shook her head. 'I asked and she said it was always clear. In fact, she said it was watery and constant, but it never got— Oh, my God.' A wild thought shot into her head, which she was tempted to dismiss instantly, but the shared look of comprehension in Cade's dark brown eyes confirmed exactly what she was thinking. 'Listen to his lungs again, please.'

'You bet.' Cade slowly and carefully moved his stethoscope around the baby's tiny rib cage.

It took everything Callie had not to interrupt and say, 'Can you hear any congestion?'

Finally, he pulled the earpieces out. 'We'll get an X-ray to confirm but, yeah, I think he's got some consolidation there.'

'It can't possibly be what we're thinking, right? I mean, he doesn't have a saddle nose.'

'Neonatal congenital syphilis?' Cade nodded. 'It's rare but it does exist in disadvantaged groups so I'm thinking, yes. I've never seen it but this little guy's mama probably didn't have any pre-natal screening or care so it's possible.'

'I'd say definitely no prenatal care.' She wished they knew who the mother was because she needed treatment too. 'I'll order full bloods, LFTs and a lumbar puncture and get him started on IV penicillin.'

'Treating him will be the easy bit,' Cade said, with a twinkle in his eye.

'What do you mean?'

His lips curved into a delicious smile. 'If the paperwork for a notifiable disease in Australia is anything like it is back home, you'll be tied up in red tape for days.'

She laughed, understanding perfectly. 'Sad but true. Thanks for your help, Cade. I'm not sure I would have got to even considering this diagnosis without you.'

'Oh, you would have,' he said, his tone genuine and complimentary, 'but I'm happy to help.' He slid his hands into his pockets to retrieve his buzzing phone and read a text message. 'I have to go. I'll catch you around, Callie.'

'Sure.' She nodded, happy to watch him walk away knowing they'd just worked together professionally and relatively painlessly.

A new beginning.

Hopefully, yes. A new beginning without the crazy attraction that had caused her so much angst.

Callie picked up the phone and called the nurse in charge of infection control. 'Lisa, it's Callie Richards. You're never going to believe this, but we've got a baby here with congenital syphilis and...'

An hour later, with all the barrier nursing in

place, Callie stripped off her gloves, having completed the last of Baby Nicols's tests—the lumbar puncture.

Scooping up all the test tubes and vials, she said to the nursing staff, 'I'll drop all these off at the lab and on my way back I'll call by the coffee cart. If you're quick, I'll take your orders and bring coffee back.'

'I can do that,' Sara Hennessey said, pulling a coffee list off the board. 'I always write one up for each shift just in case we get an offer like this.'

Callie laughed. 'That's taking organisation to a whole new level.'

'Hey,' Sara said with a steely look in her eye, 'it's coffee.'

'It's an addiction. You and Luke Stanley should form a club.'

'Oh, don't worry, we've talked about it,' Sara said, full of enthusiasm. 'As soon as he gets back, we'll be drafting members.'

'I'll think about it. Meanwhile, I'll be back in a bit.'

On her way out, Callie paused at fattening-up

corner to get her fix of now-healthy babies and to remind herself of why she did her job. Then she trekked to Pathology and ran up the stairs to the coffee cart. After handing in the order for six coffees of various permutations and combinations, she used the brewing time to browse the magazines in the nearby small gift shop. As she flicked through the pages, catching up on all the celebrity news, she reassured herself that even though she knew her pre- and post-divorce life was a mess, it looked almost functional compared with what went on in Hollywood.

'Cade, hi! You got my text?'

A beguiling female voice drifted into the shop. Callie looked up, keen to see who was talking to Cade, but the tall cluster of mobile card stands occluded her view. She couldn't see Cade or the woman with the New Zealand accent but she could hear the conversation so clearly it was as if she was part of it.

'I sure did, Natalie,' Cade replied as smoothly as ever.

Natalie? The paediatric registrar—tall, willowy, blonde and gorgeous—who'd started six months ago at the hospital was a Kiwi, and Callie was certain her name was Natalie. The woman could have modelled for a European fashion house and her arrival had generated almost as much comment from the male staff as Cade's had from the females.

'So?' Natalie almost cooed, clearly flirting. 'What do you think?'

'I think you'll look stunning in black lace,' Cade said, his deep voice caressing the words like velvet.

Black lace? Callie's hand scrunched the magazine she was holding and the shop assistant shot her a killing look. She mouthed, *'I'll buy it.'* She didn't dare speak and reveal she'd been eavesdropping. That would be far too embarrassing.

'I plan to, Cade.' Natalie's voice dropped to a sexy burr. 'That's if you like black lace. If not, I could always wear white and be the *blanc* to your *noir.* After all, there's something divine about a man in a tux.'

Callie instantly imagined Natalie's forefinger running down Cade's chest.

You don't care, okay? she told herself sternly.

It was nothing to her that Natalie was inviting Cade to the Gold Coast's A-list event at the *Palace* and it was equally nothing to her that he'd accept. One thing was certain—they'd make a stunning couple and catch the eye of photographers. She could picture them splashed all over the social pages. Cade Coleman would be in his element surrounded by the rich and the beautiful.

'It was really kind of you to think of me,' Cade said, 'but A-list events aren't really my scene.'

What? Callie wanted to knock herself on the side of the head to adjust her hearing. Was it possible that Cade was turning down both Natalie and *the* social event of the year?

'You told me you loved car racing.' Natalie's cooing voice developed an edge. 'Do you have any idea the favours I had to give out to get these tickets?'

'I'm sorry, Natalie,' Cade said gently, 'but I never asked you to get the tickets. I'm sure your efforts haven't been completely wasted. No doubt there's a long line of guys who'd be more than happy to accompany you.'

'Oh, there is,' Natalie ground out, 'but remember it's your loss.'

Incredulity poured through Callie. The fact that Cade Coleman was turning down a beautiful woman was far more significant than when he'd rejected her slightly drunken invitation at the wedding all those weeks ago.

'Okay,' Cade said. 'It's been good to see you, Natalie. I'll catch you around.'

I'll catch you around. He'd used the exact expression he'd used with her when he'd left the ward. It was his default farewell—friendly yet casually detached.

Detached.

The word slammed into her, illuminating so many things that had confused her about this charming and supposed playboy. Back in the day, his brother, Alex, had told her *he had a problem with women.* She'd taken that to mean he was a player but weeks had gone by since he'd arrived in Australia and, despite all the rumours of women throwing themselves at him, there wasn't one report that he'd actually gone on a date with anyone.

You flirted.

Sure, they had, *once*, but they hadn't dated. She'd run fast from the idea and he'd never offered. Perhaps he was running from the idea too. For the first time since she'd met him, she realised that Cade Coleman's carefree charm was a ruse. A ruse that kept people at arm's length.

It immediately begged the question, *Why?*

Luke came back inside from having put the wheelie bins out on the kerb. It was crazy how something so prosaic and mundane could be so enjoyable. For the first time in months he felt almost normal—not that he'd felt abnormal before but he'd definitely felt not quite right. During his convalescence he'd realised that for well over a year he'd assigned many of the signs of the tumour to his grief for Anna, which had effectively masked the nebulous symptoms.

Now that the bastard clump of cells was no longer in his head, he felt totally different. God, he still missed Anna, he always would, but it was more of a contained sadness than fury at himself and the world. He hadn't realised how exhausting and draining those emotions had been and he was immensely glad they were gone. He gave thanks every day that he'd been diagnosed before he'd inadvertently done any harm to his beloved daughter.

He was desperate to get back to work as soon as possible and make amends to his staff. He was determined to be the most amenable plastic surgeon ever, as well as taking them out for a meal. Nothing said *sorry and thank you* like good food and wine. He just had to clear a few hurdles first.

The fact he hadn't experienced a seizure since the one that had led to the diagnosis of the tumour was an enormous relief and with each passing day he saw the worry lines on the bridge of Chloe's nose fading. Ongoing seizures would have meant a career change, and although his good friend Tom Jordan, the neurosurgeon from Sydney Harbour Hospital, had carved out a new and successful career post-trauma, Luke was thankful he wouldn't have to do the same. He knew how tough it had been on Tom.

Luke's current hope was that at his next doctor's visit Ken Mendaz would give the *all-clear* for him to live alone again. Not that he didn't enjoy Chloe's company and presence in the cottage, he did. In three short weeks she'd managed to give his cottage a totally different feel.

The fragrant, fruity zing of her pomegranate and mango soap lingered in the bathroom, her glasses often rested on the coffee table, precariously balanced over the spine of whichever book she was reading at the time, and he didn't even want to think about the watermelon-pink lace bra and panties he'd seen fluttering on the clothesline.

To cope with his seesawing feelings about Chloe—feelings that confused the hell out of him—he tried to think of her in terms of his nurse and Amber's caregiver. When Chloe was the brisk, caring, no-nonsense woman who, like his sister Steph, verged on being bossy, he could relax. The problems started when Chloe laughed. Smiles immediately followed, wreathing her face, and then her dimples danced and her eyes sparkled with so much energy and life that he wanted to be part of it. He wanted to hold her close and inhale her joy.

Only that would dishonour Anna and complicate his friendship with Chloe, so the sooner she and her damn cute puppy moved back to her apartment, the sooner his life could return to normal.

What's normal? There's been no normal since Anna died. Chloe's real and she's here.

La, la, la, not listening. There's only ever been Anna and I still love her.

He ran his hand over his head but there was no joy to be found tugging at his hair—just the prickly feel of stubble against his palm. He spun his wedding ring on his finger. The gold band had been in position for a decade and was as much a part of him as the silver streaks in his hair. Streaks that had moved into place after Anna had died. The colour had vanished from his hair just like the colour had vanished from his life.

At least today he'd clawed back some normalcy. He'd driven his car for the first time since his surgery and his reflexes and reactions had been perfect. Chloe had suggested they take Amber to SeaWorld to celebrate this milestone and he'd agreed. They'd laughed at the antics of the seals, been awed by the sleek athleticism of the dolphins, eaten ice creams and generally enjoyed the day. It had been fun and easy, which typified most of his experiences with Chloe.

Thankfully, there'd only been one of those unexpected moments when he'd had the overwhelming urge to wrap his arms around her, haul her close and kiss her senseless.

Fortunately, for most of the time Amber, with her boundless energy, was as good an antidote to unwanted lust as cold showers. Still, Chloe moving out of the cottage would remove all temptation. He didn't want to be tempted. Hell, last week he'd almost kissed her and that would have been a disaster.

All he wanted was to live his life in a way that honoured Anna and Amber.

He latched the gate and slipped quietly back into the kitchen. As he eased the screen door closed, he heard voices drifting down the corridor. The old hall boards creaked under his feet as he walked the short distance and paused just outside the open door of his daughter's room.

'Bunny's here, Teddy's here, Clowny's here,' Chloe said.

'Amber's here.' Amber giggled at her own joke.

'She is and now it's nigh'-nigh' time,' Chloe replied with a smile in her voice as she pulled up the quilt.

''Nother story?' Amber asked hopefully.

'Your daddy read you three. Snuggle down.'

Luke grinned. Chloe did bad cop so much better than he did. Despite her protestations that she didn't know much about kids, she had the knack of settling Amber down pat. A week after his surgery they'd fallen into a routine where he bathed Amber, read her stories and kissed her goodnight.

Chloe would then put her to bed and, miracle of miracles, Amber usually settled without fuss—something she'd rarely done for him since Anna's death. Tonight was the first time he'd ever watched Chloe put Amber to bed.

His daughter obeyed Chloe's no-nonsense instructions and did indeed wriggle down until the quilt rested under her chin.

Amber peeked up at Chloe. 'Clo tell story.'

Chloe's sigh held traces of humour, as if she'd

anticipated this request and she rested her elbows on the top of the cot. 'Once upon a time there was a little girl called…'

'Amber.'

'Yes…' She laughed. 'A little girl called Amber who has a daddy who loves her very, very much.'

'Daddy hurted head.'

'He did, sweetie, but he's all better now.'

Luke listened to Amber's contributions and his breath caught in his chest at the realisation that this story was a nightly routine. Chloe must have instigated it to reassure Amber during the fraught few days he'd been in hospital.

A rush of thankfulness filled him. Chloe was utterly amazing and he owed her so much. With Steph only just leaving Arkaroola now, he didn't know how he would have managed these last three weeks without her. What did you buy someone who'd stepped into the breach without thought for herself? Neither flowers, chocolates, good wine or even a spa voucher seemed to be anywhere near enough to express his gratitude.

'Clo and Chester here,' his daughter said, clapping her little hands.

'Just for a little while.' Chloe reached out, brushing Amber's curls off her forehead before tucking bunny in close.

'Love Chester.' Amber yawned.

'Me too.'

'Love Clo.'

'Ohh.' The word came out strangled and filled with something akin to pain.

Luke shuddered and every nerve ending went on alert. Without knowing why, he strode into the room with a driving need to protect Chloe. He leaned over the cot and smiled at Amber. 'Has my girl got an extra kiss for her daddy?'

Chloe quickly stepped back and as Amber's pudgy arms wrapped themselves around his neck, he heard Chloe's footsteps leaving the room.

CHAPTER NINE

A COUPLE OF minutes later, after Luke had settled Amber, he found Chloe nestled in the corner of the couch with her feet tucked up under her—sitting the way she always did.

She looked up guiltily, her glasses flashing in the light and a glass of wine in her hand. 'Sorry.'

It was the first time he'd seen her drink any alcohol since she'd moved in. 'Don't apologise. Just because Ken's put me on the wagon for medical reasons it doesn't mean that you have to be tee-total.'

'Good.' She took close to a gulp.

He sat down next to her, worried about her reaction to Amber's childish declaration. Amber cheerfully told everyone she loved him or her, from the childcare workers to Chester. 'Everything okay? Amber not stressing you out?'

'Everything's fine,' she said over-brightly.

'Wasn't today a fabulous day? Amber's expression when the seal balanced the ball on his nose was priceless.'

He recalled that moment vividly. Their eyes had met over the top of his daughter's curly head, sharing her delight, and he'd had to stop himself from kissing Chloe. A week ago he'd brushed her cheek with his lips in an attempt at a friendly, platonic kiss—the type shared by good friends. Lust had detonated deep inside him, releasing a visceral craving for her that was so strong it had terrified him. He'd avoided touching her ever since.

He was sticking to friendship. 'Thanks for making today happen, Chloe. The picnic was delicious and you thought of everything. I think you probably had a kitchen sink in that backpack of yours.'

'I doubt that. Still, Amber's taught me that when Nick and Lucy's twins are a bit older, at least I'll be able to do the auntie thing and take them to the park and survive.'

'Hey, you remembered the nappies and the wipes and in my book that's everything.' He smiled at her, wanting to banish her brittle aura and lighten her unusually blue mood. 'One day you'll make a great mother.'

'Never going to happen.' She drained her glass and quickly refilled it, the action defiant and filled with agony.

He felt himself frown, trying to make sense of her statement. She was wonderful with Amber and she'd been equally good with the little Balinese boy, Made, all those weeks ago when he'd first met her. 'Don't you want children?'

Her top teeth pulled at her bottom lip, worrying it, and then she sighed. 'It isn't just a matter of want.'

He leaned back in the couch, understanding the modern woman's dilemma. 'You're only just thirty, Chloe. There's plenty of time for you to meet the right guy, settle down and have babies.'

A short, sharp pain jabbed him near his solar plexus and he found himself rubbing the spot, wondering what it could be.

'Meeting someone isn't the problem, Luke,' she said sharply, before standing up. 'Anyway, enough of all that. It's been a big day, I'm tired so I'll say goodnight.'

The regret on her face made him sit forward and catch her hand in his. 'You can't just say something like that and then walk away.'

'I can.' She blinked rapidly as if she was holding back tears.

'I don't want you to.' He continued holding her hand, feeling her pain hurtling into him like storm waves pounding against the uprights of a pier. 'We're friends, Chloe, and you've helped me so much. Let me help you.'

'There's nothing you can do.'

'Try me.'

She stared at him, her eyes luminous and hurting, and then she dropped her gaze to his fingers interlaced with hers. She sat down very slowly as if she really wanted to fight it and then a long silence played out.

He let her take her time.

She finally raised her head and looked at him. 'You know how nothing can ever bring Anna back to you? Not even a miracle?'

Hell, yeah. He nodded, wondering where she was going with this. 'Sure.'

'Well, same.' She was sitting so close to him that her leg lined his and her hipbone brushed his and her heat and distress flowed into him. 'No medical miracle can make me pregnant.'

He thought about her brother, Nick, who had a specialist patient list of infertile couples. Surely she knew that he had successes against all the odds and delivered babies born of women who'd experienced years of infertility. There was always hope.

He wanted to throw her a bone to lessen her pain. Squeezing her hand, he said, 'Don't rule anything out, Chloe. The human body is amazingly resilient.'

She closed her eyes and sagged against him for the briefest moment before sitting up straight again. 'Resilience won't help a damn, Luke. I had a hysterectomy at sixteen.'

His jaw dropped. Of all the things he'd anticipated she might say, this wasn't one of them.

Chloe registered the flash of shock in Luke's eyes and followed its trajectory across his high cheeks before it buried itself in his dark stubble. Why had she blurted out her secret? Why had she told him? She didn't tell *anyone* and Luke certainly didn't need to know. It wasn't like they had a future together—take one infertile woman and one grieving widow and mix… Nope, not a good combination, no matter which way you looked at it.

But you've told him. It's out there, so deal with it.

She steeled herself for the anticipated questions, for the probable censure and disapproval, and the change in his behaviour towards her. She knew the drill. She'd been there, done that and got the T-shirt. First with her father and more recently with Jason. His horrified expression combined with the way he'd stepped back from her so fast—as if she had leprosy—was burned on her soul.

Luke's eyes darkened to mossy green and then he silently wrapped his arms around her, pulling her in close.

She gave in to the unexpected hug and buried her face in his shoulder, absorbing his empathy and appreciating that he wasn't offering her any platitudes. He probably knew how worthless they really were, having heard them all when his wife had died. The slow, strong, rhythmic beat of his heart thudded against her chest and she wanted to stay there, snuggled into him, for ever. Safe, warm and not judged.

You need to move.

The elapsed time had now passed *normal support* and was fast moving into the *getting-awkward* stage.

She raised her head and noticed the big, damp spot on his shoulder. 'I've made your shirt all wet. Sorry.'

'No problem. Amber's done a lot worse.' He smiled and reached for her wine, passing it to her with his left hand and leaving his right arm loosely slung around her shoulders. The light played off his wedding ring.

He still hadn't asked her why such a tragedy had befallen her and that unnerved her. The unasked question was like the click of a landmine— it was going to go off, but exactly when she had no clue.

Sipping the *sauvignon blanc*, she vacillated on what to do or say next but the weight and wonderful warmth of his arm around her was draining her brain. Staring straight ahead, she decided to explode the landmine herself. 'On the few occasions I've told people, they usually have questions.'

His fingers played with her hair. 'Of course I want to know why you needed such catastrophic surgery at such a young age but I also get it if you don't want to tell me.'

He understands.

Relief flowed into her. He'd met grief head-on, just like she had. He knew the massive chasms that could suck you down, trapping you in darkness whenever you dared revisit places that haunted you.

Maybe it was that understanding, maybe it was the caring warmth of his arm against her or even the relaxing effects of the wine—did it matter? No, but for some inexplicable reason she wanted to tell him.

She moistened her lips. 'It's not a quick story.'

He gently squeezed the top of her arm and his

insightful gaze rested on her. 'I've got all the time in the world.'

She took in a deep breath and started. 'My parents are Greek, traditionalists and strict. My mother is scared of my father and my father rules the family with a will of iron...'

Luke kept his arm around Chloe, hearing her soft voice, listening to her story and wishing desperately that she didn't have a story to tell because he knew it was going to be hellishly bad. No gynaecologist would remove a sixteen-year-old's uterus unless he had no other choice. Unless it was to prevent her death.

'Nick, as the first born,' Chloe continued, 'was the golden boy who could do no wrong—and, unlike me, he never did. I love him dearly and sadly my actions cost him a lot. Unlike me, he toed the family line, obeying my father, working hard at school and generally doing what was asked of him.'

He stroked her ear. 'It's my understanding that in Greek families it's often a lot easier to be male.'

The flecks of brown in her eyes shone starkly

against the khaki green and she gave a small nod of agreement. 'My father has certain beliefs about how women should be raised and educated. At the end of year ten he refused to re-enrol me at school. I was bereft. I tried pleading, crying, throwing things. You name it, I did it, but it was useless. Nothing Nick, my mother, the principal or I could say or do would change his mind. Legally, I could leave school.'

His utter shock at a child having her education stolen from her must have shone on his face because she gave him a wan smile.

'It's archaic, I know. My father had my life planned out according to what he considered was best for me. As well as helping *Mama* at home, he ordered me to work in my uncle's fish and chip shop. I hated that job almost as much as I hated my father, but there was one positive...' She shrugged. 'Well, at least, at barely sixteen I thought it was a positive.'

'What was that?'

'I got to walk to and from the shop each day, which gave me fifteen minutes of blessed freedom there and back. My Anglo friends fell into two camps. Those who thought I was incredibly lucky to be out of school and those who couldn't understand. Rick, a good mate, fell into the "*couldn't understand*" camp and he'd meet me in the park to give me books and homework pages so I could try and keep up. Nick helped too.'

He'd always liked Nick Kefes. 'He's a good man, your brother.'

'Beyond good.' She blew her nose and blinked rapidly. 'I got away with doing schoolwork at home for six months until my father found my stash of books and went ballistic, including scaring Rick so much that he was too petrified to help me again. From then on I was escorted to and from the shop but my father couldn't control the people I met while I was working and I met Darren, an apprentice carpenter. I started sneaking out at night to meet him.'

She gave a short, tight laugh. 'He was my knight in shining armour, promising me that he'd save me from my life and we'd move in together. We were just kids but I was so desperate to get away from home I believed him. To cut a long story short, we had sex and I got pregnant.'

Her tone reminded him of when he told people about the car accident. *Anna died.* Emotionless, detached, pragmatic. It was the only way to tell the story without breaking down.

He wanted her to know he understood. 'That must have been terrifying for you.'

'At first it wasn't because I truly believed that Darren would take care of me. It took me a couple of months to even realise I was pregnant so I was twelve weeks before I told him. He promised me everything would be fine and then he disappeared and never contacted me again. I didn't believe that he was gone for good so I waited a few weeks and then panic set in.

'I was seventeen weeks pregnant, I had no money, no friends, and my mother and brother had limited resources to help me. And I knew my father would throw me out of the house if he ever found out. It was the first time in my life I realised I was utterly alone. I visited a clinic and had a late-term abortion.'

She shuddered against him and he immediately

pulled her back in close against his shoulder and pressed a kiss into her hair. 'It sounds like you didn't have a choice.'

She sucked in her lips, her jaw tight as if she was readying to get the next bit of the story over and done with as fast as possible. 'I went home after the termination, told my mother I had a heavy period and went to bed. The pain was excruciating and I truly thought I was dying. I didn't realise that I was. When Nick came home from doing my shift at the shop, I was almost unconscious and half my circulating blood volume was in the bed. He called an ambulance and I arrested on the way in.'

Her voice became the one she used at work—brisk, factual and professional. 'For most people a termination of pregnancy is very safe but I was unlucky. My uterine wall was very thin and the procedure perforated it. To save me, they had to sacrifice—'

'Your uterus,' Luke interrupted, wanting to save her from having to say it.

She nodded. 'And things went to hell after that. My father, having had the doctor at the hospital explain to him the reason why his daughter had almost died, kicked me out of the house the day I was discharged home. He met me at the front door with my bag packed. I'd shamed the family.'

Luke thought of Amber and his heart cramped in his chest. How could any father do that to their child? 'Surely Nick helped you?'

Her eyes swam with tears. 'Nick saved me. When our father refused to have me home, Nick left too. We spent a few weeks in emergency housing and then, with both of us working in menial jobs, we managed to get a flat. The fact Nick passed his year twelve that year is testament to his brilliance.

'I was barely functioning on any level, but I feared being homeless more than anything so I kept working. I cleaned houses, I waited on tables and did pretty much anything I could to earn money. I owed Nick so much and I happily worked two jobs to help him get through six years of medical school. Three years after that, when he started his obstetrics specialisation, I enrolled at university and started nursing.

'It was the best thing I ever did and in the last

couple of years I've really found my feet.' She shot him a look that said, *Don't disagree with me.* 'I'm happy and content.'

He wasn't convinced. 'You're a great nurse and I'm glad for you that you love your job. But you do know that there's more than one way to have a child. Plenty of couples adopt.'

She stiffened as if he'd hit her. 'I used to think that way too,' she said tartly, 'right up until two years ago when my then fiancé broke off our engagement because I was incapable of giving him his *own* child.'

Luke wanted to hit the unnamed bastard. 'You deserve so much better than that, Chloe.'

She shrugged. 'Yes, well, it's a moot point really, so it doesn't matter.'

'Don't say that.' His words rushed out, hating it that she sounded so resigned. 'You're beautiful, bright and vivacious. Any decent guy would be lucky to have you.'

She turned and lifted her gaze to his, doubt shimmering in her eyes. 'What planet do you live on, Luke? I'm damaged goods.'

He wanted to blast out her doubt and her cynicism, make her realise how truly beautiful and amazing she was and how much she deserved to be loved. Only he knew how inadequate words could be. How little they did to help when life threw up moments of immeasurable cruelty, and how easy it was to dismiss and discard them. No, words were useless here. This needed action.

Without pausing to think, he lowered his head and kissed her.

Luke's lips touched Chloe's so very lightly that for a fleeting moment she thought she must be imagining the connection. Her mind had to be creating the idea of him kissing her and fulfilling a long-held dream, because there was no way it could possibly be real.

Her tongue traced the edges of her bottom lip and she tasted a hint of mint and a *soupçon* of musk—the flavours of Luke. Then the tip of her tongue registered a different feel—his lips. Flavours met fire, her entire body lit up with blinding need and she opened her mouth and took him as hers.

She heard a guttural moan in the back of his throat, and in it she recognised longing, wanting and lust that perfectly matched her own. Her hands reached out, pressing against him, feeling the strong musculature of his chest underneath the soft cotton of his shirt. She spread her fingers, needing the touch to believe this was really happening.

His hands cupped her cheeks, tilting her head, angling her mouth to his, and then he deepened the kiss. His tongue caressed her mouth so gently and so reverently that one tiny part of her wanted to cry. The rest of her was too busy riding the waves of wonder, joy and rising desire to think at all.

His lips and tongue roved over her mouth, finding the special places that directed the spinning rafts of tingles zipping in her veins straight to her core. He captured her moans of sheer delight with his mouth and returned them to her more potent than before. She needed to feel him, all of him, and she wrapped her arms around his neck and in the process knocked her glasses against his head.

'Ouch.' He laughed, rubbing his temple where her frames had dug into him.

'Sorry.' She put her fingers over his.

He stared at her through glazed eyes.

She held her breath, cursing her glasses for breaking the moment and waiting for him to realise they'd been kissing each other like a couple who'd been given two minutes to live. Waiting for sanity to move into his out-of-focus gaze and pull him away from her completely. The way it had every other time they'd shared a sexually charged moment.

You can be the one to stop this right now.

I don't want to.

And she didn't. It had been so long since she'd been made to feel like a desirable woman that she didn't want to let the feelings go. She was no fool. She certainly didn't have stars in her eyes that this meant anything more than the two of them giving in to the lust that had shimmered and spun between them for weeks. It wasn't a future—it was just *now*.

He smiled at her. Her heart sang and then everything went into slow motion. He reached out his hands and slid her glasses off her face, discarding them on the coffee table. Then he gently dragged the hair-tie from her ponytail and ran his hands through her hair, smoothing it down before carefully bringing it over her shoulders. 'That's better. Now I can see your beautiful eyes.'

Bringing his head down close, he kissed her eyelids with such delicacy that as her head fell back she cried out from the sheer joy of it. As he lowered her on the couch, she slid her hand between the placket of his shirt, the backs of her fingers brushing his skin. Shocks of wonder rocked her and she pulled him down with her.

He trailed kisses from her jaw to her hairline, before burying his face in her hair. 'You smell like a tropical fruit basket.'

She laughed. 'Is that a good thing?'

He rose up on his arms and stared down at her, desire hot and glittering in his eyes. 'Absolutely.'

'You smell like salt and sunshine,' she said, un-buttoning his shirt.

'Is that a bad thing?'

She pushed his shirt off his shoulders and mar-velled at the view. 'I'm not complaining.' Rising up, she pressed kisses to his sternum, tracing her tongue along his skin—sucking, licking and tasting—the heady combination making the muscles between her legs twitch. She was desperate to feel him inside her.

He shuddered at the touch of her mouth and she wanted to high-five someone. Anyone. She wanted to call out to the world that she'd made that happen. Luke Stanley wanted her. *Her.*

The muscles on his arms bulged as he pushed up from her and shucked his shirt. Then he leaned back on his haunches and grinned, his face alight with desire and devoid of all the strain and pain she always associated with him. 'Someone's overdressed.'

His long and dextrous fingers whipped her T-shirt over her head and then his gaze shot straight to her aqua and black lace bra. He groaned. 'Do you have any idea how tough it's been, seeing your underwear on my clothesline and imagining what it looks like on you?'

Her nipples puckered in delight that he'd been working as hard as she had to fight the attraction between them, but a niggle of worry made her say, 'Sometimes reality doesn't live up to expectation.'

His fingers traced the black lace that decorated the edge of the bra and brushed the swell of her breast. 'The reality's more than fine, Chloe.' He lowered his mouth and suckled her through the lace.

White light streaked through her and she bucked against him, feeling his erection through his jeans.

'If you like that, then you might like this.' He focused his attention on her other breast until she was writhing under him and desperate to get rid of the bra so she could fully enjoy the hot and wet ministrations of his mouth against her tight and begging skin.

She pushed at his chest. 'Take it off. Now. Please.'

'Anything you say.' He reached one hand around and fumbled with the clasps.

The bra didn't move and the thought that he was out of practice flitted across her mind. She batted it away—fast—not wanting to think about the reason why he was out of practice. Real life didn't belong here. This was just a moment in time between two people who needed to lose themselves in each other.

The bra finally fell away. She dropped it on the floor next to his shirt and immediately wrapped her fingers around his belt. 'Let's get rid of everything, then, shall we?'

'I like the way you think.'

He kissed her hot, hard and fast as she pushed his pants off his hips and down his legs so he could kick them off.

Neither of them had factored in shoes and one moment he was kissing her and the next he was on the floor. Half laughing and half concerned, she managed to splutter out, 'Are you okay?'

He rubbed his hip and gave a wry smile. Grabbing her hand, he said, 'I'm too old for couch sex and you deserve better. Come on.'

'Just a sec.' She reached for her shirt, suddenly embarrassed she had to run to his bedroom half-naked.

'Oh, no,' he said, his fingers flicking the shirt out of her grasp. 'No one is getting dressed.' The next moment she found herself hefted over his shoulder, held in place by one of his hands deliciously splayed over her bikini-clad bottom. Lucky for her, the thin silk did nothing to shield her from the heat of his palm and the gentle and delicious kneading of his fingers.

As he strode down the hall and entered his bedroom, she trailed her hands down his naked back until she slid them underneath the elastic of his boxer shorts, cupping his buttocks.

He stopped with a jerk. 'Do you want me to drop you?' he asked, his voice gravelly with desire.

'Only if you fall with me.'

He lowered her carefully and then, like a jet-black panther, he crawled slowly up the bed, his moss-green eyes fixed on her face. As he moved, he trailed the forefinger of his right hand up the arch of her foot, along her shin, across her inner thigh. Just as he got close to the apex of her thighs and she was breathing out, *'Oh, yes, please,'* he skirted the sensitive area and traced his finger around her hip. From there he skated it across her belly until it came to rest between her breasts. Her skin burned for more of the addictive and erotic touch.

Now he was straddling her, his lean body all corded muscle, taut tendons and thick, blue veins.

Powerful and strong, he hovered over her, trembling with leashed tension ready to be cut loose on her, but she had no fear. He was beautiful. She wanted him so much but well-honed survival skills kicked in despite the risk that it would bring his past flooding back and ruin everything.

She raised her hand and cupped his cheek. 'Condoms?'

A muscle tensed in his jaw. 'I don't have any.'

She held his gaze. 'It's not a problem unless you have something.'

'I'm fine,' he said abruptly.

The next moment his lips pressed hard against hers and she lost her breath to him, as if he needed it more than she did. His tongue lashed her mouth—taking and giving, searching and finding. His desperate need for her overpowered everything, as hers did for him.

Her body sought his, pressing against him, feeling his length mould to hers and yet wanting to be even closer. Her hands roved all over his back, caressing, exploring, finding the dips and the crevices and committing them to memory.

Wanting this to last for ever but knowing it was just one moment in time.

His mouth dropped down her belly, his tongue swirling around her belly button stud as his fingers found her aching, throbbing clitoris. She gasped, thrashing underneath him.

'Am I hurting you?' Concern stopped his fingers.

'God, no, it's amazing.' She moistened her lips at the touch she'd never known from a man before, and was amazed at how much her body begged for it. 'Keep going.'

His deep and melodic laugh rained over her as his fingers worked their magic. Whirls of sensation built on each other, each strand intensifying the delight until she lost touch with the sights and sounds of the room and with the feel of the mattress against her back. The only thing that existed were his fingers on her and the agonising ecstasy that surged through her, demanding she ride it to the peak and be willingly thrown wherever it took her.

Lights danced across her vision as her head whipped from side to side. Control slipped utterly and she screamed his name. As she shattered into a river of bliss, his mouth covered hers, sharing the moment.

She broke the kiss and gripped his shoulders. 'Thank you.'

He smiled gently. 'You're welcome.'

She pushed his shoulder, rolling him over and going with him. 'I think that deserves a return favour.'

His fingers drew circles on her buttocks. A muscle twitched in his cheek. 'Can I choose the favour?'

A shiver shot through her at what he might suggest. 'Maybe.'

He whispered in her ear and she relaxed. 'No problem.'

After all, he'd just given her the best orgasm of her life and she trusted him implicitly.

She rose up on all fours and his hands massaged her back and her breasts, making her body sing before he gently entered her, the length of him filling her completely. She sighed at how good it felt. His lips touched the middle of her back as he started to move slowly and she met each thrust with her own.

I can't see his face.

The thought skittered across her mind before vanishing quickly as her body took over. Their rhythm gained momentum and their bodies became one, driving each other forward until, with a cry, they spun out on a stream of fulfilment and then collapsed, utterly sated.

CHAPTER TEN

LUKE LAY ON his back, panting and staring at the ceiling.

What have I just done?

Guilt burrowed in. He'd just had sex with a woman who wasn't his wife. What had started as a quick kiss to show Chloe that she was very much a desirable woman had ended in mind-blowing sex.

He rubbed his palms across his face, feeling the edge of his wedding ring drag against his cheek. *I'm sorry, Anna.*

Twice he could have called a halt, apologised to Chloe and walked away. He'd been given two perfect opportunities—his for the taking—and he'd ignored them, letting his body drive the agenda, deaf to reason. Sex with Chloe was the last thing either of them needed in their messed-up lives, so why had he done it?

Because it's been a damn long time, his body chimed in, stirring again as Chloe's legs tangled with his. *You're a healthy, red-blooded male.*

God, he'd forgotten how amazing sex could be—the rush of euphoria followed by the feeling of contentment that now swam in his veins.

Chloe rolled against him, her hair tickling his nostrils with that intoxicating, fresh scent, which invigorated him every time he inhaled it. 'I'm guessing maybe you haven't had sex in a while.'

He gazed down at her, into a face filled with concern for him, and his heart both ached and squeezed. It unnerved him and he didn't want to think about it. 'Did you think I was out of practice?' he joked, trying to keep the conversation light.

She trailed her fingers across his chest. 'Your clothing removal's a little rusty so you lost points there.'

'Is that so?' He captured her hand in his. 'And for overall performance?'

'Let me see...' She cocked her head as if she was giving it serious thought. 'The judges gave you nine point nine.'

He grinned at her, ridiculously pleased. 'Not so rusty after all.'

'Not where it counts, no.'

She rested her head on his shoulder and he automatically pressed a kiss into her hair. It felt companionable and uncomplicated. Nice.

'This is the first time you've had sex since Anna died, isn't it?'

The words slammed into him, making him flinch, and his throat tightened.

She raised her head, her gaze demanding an answer. 'Luke?'

He closed his eyes and the blurry image of his beloved wife appeared, so he opened them again. Fast. 'Yes.'

'It was just sex, Luke,' she said matter-of-factly.

He felt himself frowning. 'What do you mean, just sex?'

She chewed her lip. 'Exactly that. Two adults taking a moment because they both needed it. Sex can be simple, you know. Casual. It doesn't have to have strings attached.'

The weight of age and time bore down on him. 'I never did that.'

Chloe sat up fast—shock and surprise making her feel dizzy. As she pulled the sheet up under her arms, her mind roved over what he'd just said. She'd been leading the conversation, trying to check out if Luke was okay because although she'd never experienced the death of a partner, she was certain that the first time he had sex with someone other than his wife might trigger some tough emotions. She hadn't counted on his lack of experience before he'd committed to Anna. 'You've never had casual sex before?'

His expression mixed sadness with an element of being offended. He pushed up and rested his back against the headboard, his broad and beautiful chest on full view. 'I met Anna in my final year of high school and we started dating. We lost our virginity to each other after our exams.

'I imagine our families thought the relationship would flounder soon enough but we'd applied to the same university college so being separated by geography wasn't an issue. When she finished her economics degree, we moved in together. Four years after that, during my residency, we got married. I loved being married,' he said with a sad smile, 'so, yeah, I'm a one-woman guy.'

She tried not to let his probably unintentional barb pierce her as she wrapped her mind around the sort of relationship he and Anna had shared. 'That's a big love,' she said faintly, hating the way her voice sounded. She'd never experienced anything like it.

'Yeah.'

He stared out into the distance with his *Anna look* and her entire body ached. Why had she asked if she was the first woman since Anna? She could have just enjoyed the sex, said *thank you* and returned to her own room. But, no, she'd gone and brought his late wife into bed with them.

Great going, Chloe. You suck at everything to do with men. Make an excuse and leave now.

She opened her mouth to speak but Luke spoke first. 'So this sex with no strings attached...' his green eyes sparkled, partially obscuring the permanent sadness that lingered there '...is it something you might be interested in?'

Keep safe and say no.

His gaze implored and every good intention

inside her started to crumble, one resolution at a time. She sought to find a way it might work for both of them, knowing what they'd both experienced at the hands of life. A way to keep her heart contained and intact. 'I'm not looking for a relationship, Luke.'

He nodded. 'Exactly. Neither am I.'

'So no commitment, no regrets?'

'Are you up for that?'

Yes. 'Maybe.'

'Maybe?' He grinned, reaching for her. 'Seeing you refined and defined my offer, I'm taking that as a *yes.*'

She raised a brow. 'And that's your seduction technique?'

He pulled her into his arms and ran his tongue along her collarbone before dipping into the hollow at her throat.

Her head fell back and her breasts rubbed deliciously against his chest, pebbling into tingling nubs.

He nuzzled her décolletage. 'How am I doing?'

Her breath sped up, pulling in and out, hard and fast as her body liquefied. 'Keep…practising.'

He laughed—a wicked, deep, sensual sound—and then he did exactly what she'd told him.

Amber was sitting at Luke's feet, stacking plastic containers from the big kitchen drawer. He marvelled at how something so simple and easy could give such enjoyment and he wondered why she had a boxful of expensive toys when all it took was this. He'd noticed that Chloe often pulled the drawer out when Amber was weary and fractious, and it was always a hit.

He wasn't immune to the irony that a childless woman had taught him more about his daughter than he'd been able to teach her.

As Amber played, Luke and Chloe cooked dinner. Or, to be more precise, Chloe was cooking and he was cheerfully being a kitchen hand, following instructions and dicing all the vegetables for the stir-fry. A week had passed since the night a consoling kiss had catapulted them into bed together and although Chloe always returned to her bed around midnight, they started every evening in his. He wondered why he'd been so fearful that sex would cause complications. This *no commit-*

ment, no regrets idea of hers was an unexpected gift and it had gone a long way towards lessening his guilt about Anna.

This wasn't love. It was sex—pure and simple. It might have taken him seventeen years to discover casual sex but he was now making up for lost time.

It's not really casual when it's just with one person.

He turned the volume down on his conscience and poured Chloe a glass of wine. 'I was thinking—'

'Sounds dangerous,' Chloe quipped with a smile as she set the wok on the gas burner. She loved this time of day, with both of them in the kitchen, working together, Amber close by and Chester in his basket.

He grinned at her. 'Very funny. I've been thinking that it's time to start the ball rolling towards me returning to work, and that starts with me doing a full day at home alone.'

Her hand tightened on the spatula as her heart cramped. *This is it. The real world is bursting your bubble of denial.* 'So you need me to move out?'

'God, no.' He wrapped his arm around her waist and kissed her swiftly.

She hated the relief that trickled through her on the coat-tails of desire. 'What then?'

'Well, I was thinking if you go back to work and Amber goes back to daycare, I can run the house and meet you at the end of the day with a glass of wine and a basic meal.'

'The wine idea is tempting,' she teased.

'If you're horrified at the thought of my cooking, feel free to take over,' he said without heat.

She ran the logistics through her head. 'What about when I'm rostered on lates? Can you cope with dinner and the bewitching hour with Amber?'

His face sobered. 'That's the real test. I need to be able to cope with that before I can even think about dealing with patients and surgery.'

'True.'

'So, what do you think?'

Post-surgery, with his sister away, he'd needed Chloe's help. Now, with every passing day he needed it less and less, but he wasn't pushing her to leave and he was asking her opinion of his plans. Did it mean something?

Don't overthink this.

'I think it sounds like a plan. I'll call Keri.'

He kissed her again—long and slow—as if sealing the deal.

'Daddy.' Amber tugged on both their legs. 'Up. Me cuddle.'

Abruptly, he pulled away from Chloe and scooped his daughter into his arms. 'Who's my best girl?' He kissed her curls.

Chloe's heart did a ridiculous lurch.

No commitment and no regrets, remember?

Catching the glint of Luke's wedding ring, it was impossible to forget.

'How's Luke?'

Keri rushed up to Chloe the moment her feet hit the shiny linoleum floor of the ward.

'When's he coming back?' Kate asked, now visibly pregnant and wearing a voluminous maternity uniform.

The pang Chloe normally experienced on seeing a pregnant woman didn't sting nearly as much as it usually did, but as Keri and Kate started firing questions at her, she didn't have a moment to reflect on it.

'He's doing really well,' she said with a smile. 'If everything goes according to plan, he'll be back here in less than two months.'

'Wow, that's amazing. People usually take at least three months to recover from brain surgery,' Kate said.

'Yes, but they don't have me looking after them,' Chloe quipped, ready to steer the conversation around to ward work. She was doing a nine a.m. to three p.m. shift today to cover the busiest hours.

'You did an amazing thing, taking on looking after Luke and his little girl,' Keri said. 'Especially with how you feel about children. I bet you're glad to be back at work.'

Am I? Dropping Amber off at daycare had been fraught. She could still feel the little girl's arms clinging to her and her sobs ringing in her ears. The childcare worker had extricated Amber and mouthed, *'Just go.'*

Chloe, blinking back tears, had done just that

but part of her heart had stayed behind. The moment she'd parked the car in the hospital car park, she'd telephoned to check on Amber. The carer had reassured her that Amber had settled quickly and was busy talking about Chester.

Chester was spending the day with Luke and she wondered how Luke was faring with the grocery shopping and the installation of the new dishwasher he'd bought. Chester was probably stealing the grey hoses and Luke would be yelling at him and cuddling him at the same time. She stifled a smile, thinking about how he let her dog get away with just about everything. She really needed to get Chester back into his training regime or he'd end up being a huge dog with no manners.

After a month of the three of them living side by side and sharing everything, today she felt as if she was missing a limb. Although she hadn't even started her shift, she couldn't wait to get home and share her day and hear all about his.

The cottage isn't home. Your dusty apartment is home.

But it was getting harder and harder to remind herself of that.

Chloe mustered up a bright smile for Keri and Kate, deciding to take the easy option and not disabuse them of their thoughts about her and children. 'You're right. After four weeks of chasing around after a toddler, coming back to work will be a relief and a rest.'

Liar, liar, pants on fire.

Keri's smile wavered slightly. 'We're just glad our career nurse is back.'

Is that what I am? For the first time in a long time her beloved job didn't hold quite the same allure.

As Chloe slid her key into the lock on the cottage door, the shrill chirping of the cicadas stopped and she could hear the gentle wash of the waves against the beach. It was a dark, windless night and she'd just worked her first late shift since returning to work five days ago. Tiptoeing quietly into the sleeping house, she slipped off her shoes and went directly to the shower to wash off the ward. Experience with Luke's hot-water service had taught her to run the shower for a full minute before she got in, rather than doing a freezing St Vitus dance in the cubicle.

She turned on the taps and then stripped off her clothes. She was just dumping everything into the laundry hamper when arms went around her waist. She jumped in surprise and then a very familiar body pressed against her back. Luke's skin touched her spine and silk boxers caressed her behind.

His lips nuzzled her neck. 'I missed you.'

Joy poured through her and she put her hand up behind her and touched his head. 'I'm here now and I'm all yours as soon as I've had a shower.'

'I thought I might join you.'

A thrill of anticipation shot through her and she turned in his arms to face him. 'That sounds perfect.'

He grinned, shucked his boxers and joined her in the shower. It wasn't a large shower, and it was impossible to turn around without their bodies touching, but she wasn't complaining one little bit.

Grabbing her shower mitt, he squirted coconut-scented gel on it. Starting at her shoulders, he used the mitt in circular motions across her back before he tossed it aside and pressed his thumbs into the tight muscles of her shoulders.

'Busy shift?'

She sighed at the delicious, relaxing touch that was making coherent thought difficult. 'Tough shift. Burn victims. The youngest is eight.'

'Hell.'

She heard his concern and his frustration that he hadn't been there. 'In another month you'll be back at work, dealing with it all.'

'It can't go fast enough.'

His hands moved down her back and those talented fingers, which could stitch the tiniest vessels together, pressed firmly against each vertebra of her spine and massaged the connected muscles and tendons. It was all she could do to stay standing.

'I had no idea you had this talent.'

He kissed her shoulder. 'I have hidden depths.'

She laughed. 'You just want to get lucky.'

'Is it working?'

She imagined the twinkle in his eyes and the

grin on his face and her heart swelled. 'Keep on going and I'll let you know.'

The warm water cascaded over them and his hands reached her buttocks. She pressed against his hands, wanting their touch and hoping they would slide between her legs, because she knew he was particularly good at that, but after a brief but wonderful massage his hands fell away.

She opened her eyes to see him reaching for her shampoo and the next moment his hands were in her hair, washing it and caressing her scalp. Then he reached around her and washed her breasts and her belly. Half of her wanted to turn around, wrap her arms around his neck and her legs around his waist and feel him deep inside her, but his touch was so tender and thoughtful that she didn't want it to stop.

A sob rose in her throat.

This touch wasn't sexual—it was full of caring and reverence. Her parents had abandoned her and Jason hadn't loved her enough. Nick was wonderful and cared for her but it hadn't been like this. This was something in an utterly different sphere.

This is love.

I love him.

The thought exploded in her head, freezing her breath in her lungs and cramping her heart.

No. How did I let this happen?

Despite everything she'd told herself about holding back and keeping her heart safe, she'd fallen in love with Luke. Deeply and irrevocably in love.

Unaware that her life had just turned upside down, he turned off the shower, guided her out onto the waiting mat, towelled her dry and then wrapped her in an enormous, fluffy bath sheet.

Falling in love with him might not be a disaster, her endorphin-infused brain told her as her body whimpered, limp with need and with the wondrous emotions of feeling treasured. She kissed him. 'Thank you. That has to be the best coming-home-from-work welcome I've ever had in my life.'

Dark green eyes gazed down at her and he took her hand. 'I haven't finished yet.'

He led her to his room, lowered her onto the bed and using the combination of his mouth and hands selflessly took her to the dizzying heights of bliss. As she floated back down his hands started to turn her over but she stopped him. Cupping his cheeks, she said, 'I'd like to try something different.'

His face took on a guarded look. 'O…kay.'

She rolled him over and straddled him, wanting to see the face of the man she loved shatter in ecstasy when she took him to that amazing place. Wanting him to watch her taking him there.

Gently lowering herself over him, she sighed as he filled her, his shaft rubbing that sensitive place where she craved to be touched. She moved her hips, creating the friction she knew he'd love and anticipated his thrusts meeting hers.

He didn't move.

Her hands touched his chest. 'Luke?'

His lust-glazed gaze collided with her shoulder. 'Hmm?'

'Is this working for you?'

He didn't reply.

She leaned down and kissed him—long and deep, using her tongue against his mouth just how he liked it.

He groaned and thrust into her, slowly at first but quickly gaining both length and speed.

She tore her mouth away from his and matched him thrust for thrust, riding him and taking him higher and higher and closer to release.

His breathing quickened and she recognised from the sounds that he was close. As her body screamed for her mind to let go, she fought it, wanting him to orgasm first. She gazed down at his face. He shattered with his eyes closed and his face turned away from her.

Her heart ripped and bled.

CHAPTER ELEVEN

'OH, MY GOD, look at your hair!'

Luke's sister Steph had just jumped out of her family's four-wheel drive and was staring at him in his driveway. She threw her arms around him, squeezing him so tightly that he could barely breathe. 'We've been so worried.'

He patted her back appreciatively. 'No need for that. I told you I was fine.'

She sniffed against his shoulder. 'I know, but I never believed you.' She drew back and recovered herself, wiping her tears away with the back of her hand. 'Marty, girls,' she called into the vehicle. 'Come and give Luke a great, big hug.'

Squeals of delight were quickly followed by arms being wrapped around his knees, hips and waist. He hugged and kissed his nieces, thanking each of them for the drawings they'd sent him.

Marty slapped him on the back and pumped his hand. 'You're looking good, mate.'

'I feel good.' And he did. Really good. Better than he'd felt since— He stalled the thought, not prepared to go there.

'That tumour really did a number on you,' Steph said thoughtfully. 'You've looked so grey and drawn for so long and now look at you.' She smiled broadly. 'You're glowing and happy.' Glancing around, she said, 'Where's my gorgeous niece?'

'Napping.'

'Whoa, bro'. Amber's having an afternoon nap? You really *are* on top of things.'

He was about to mention Chloe when Elspeth squealed.

'Mummy, look!'

'Aw, he's so cute,' Lexie said, breaking into a run.

'Can I hold him? Please?' Jess, the youngest of the three girls, pleaded.

His nieces had spied Chester, who'd somehow managed to escape into the garden.

'You've got a dog?' The rising inflection of Steph's voice matched the incredulity on her face.

He shook his head. 'He's Chloe's dog, but Amber's convinced Chester is her own personal property.'

'Oh, is Chloe still here?' Steph asked, interest clear in her gaze.

As if on cue, the screen door swung open and Chloe stepped out. Her chestnut hair swung around her face, some curls catching on the arms of her glasses, and she looked beautiful, tanned and relaxed, wearing a pink silk top and green shorts.

Steph punched him in the arm. 'No wonder you're looking so happy.'

Guilt and pleasure pummelled him, the mixture leaving an odd taste in his mouth. 'We're just friends, Steph.'

That would be friends with benefits.

No way in hell was he elaborating on *that* to his sister.

Steph raised her brows. 'Maybe you should be more.'

'Don't go there, okay?' he ground out tersely. 'If you promise to behave, I'll introduce you.'

Steph laughed and, completely ignoring him, walked straight up to Chloe.

Chloe, who'd been on tenterhooks inside, agonising over whether she should wait until Luke brought his family in to meet her or whether she should take the bull by the horns and introduce herself, had her dilemma solved for her when Chester escaped.

Butterflies batted her stomach and she hated how nervous she felt about meeting the Markham family. Now Luke's sister was making a beeline for her. Chloe sucked in a deep breath and extended her hand. 'You must be Steph. It's lovely to finally meet you.'

'None of that handshaking stuff,' Steph said, moving straight in for a hug. 'We can't thank you enough for what you've done for Luke and Amber.'

The warmth and affection in Steph's hug made Chloe's throat tight. This family who barely knew her, valued her. 'No problem. I was happy to help out.'

Luke appeared and inserted himself between them. He casually slung one arm over his sister's shoulder and the other around Chloe's waist in a familiar affectionate gesture that he often used with her.

'Time for coffee,' he said.

Resisting the urge to drop her head on his shoulder, she said, 'Steph might want tea.'

'Nah,' he said, 'she wants coffee.'

Chloe rolled her eyes. 'You just want to show off that new machine of yours.'

'She's got you pegged, bro'.' Steph elbowed Luke in the ribs in a sisterly way. 'Marty can't wait to show you his new diff lock.' She shot Chloe a conspiratorial look. 'Boys and their toys.''

'Enough of that sexist talk, thank you very much,' Luke said, with a twinkle in his eye, 'or you can make your own coffee.'

'That's far too serious a threat to ignore, Steph,' Chloe said, teasingly. She pulled open the screen door. 'The sad thing is that not only is he full of himself about his coffee prowess, he does actually make fabulous coffee.'

'I'm the perfect man.' Luke winked at her and

gave her hand a quick squeeze before walking into the kitchen.

Her heart cramped. *I know you are, and that's my biggest problem.*

An hour later, after everyone had eaten their fill of fruit, cake and coffee, Luke met Chloe in the hall as she was coming out of the bathroom. Trapping her between himself and the wall, he leaned, closed his eyes and kissed her.

The thrill that shot through her every time he did that hadn't diminished over time. If anything, it had intensified despite the warning voice in the back of her mind that loving him was dangerous because he couldn't love her back.

'The kids are desperate to go to the beach so we thought we'd head down now. Will you come too?'

'Sure, but you guys go now and I'll come down when I've cleared up the food and stacked the dishwasher.'

He tucked some strands of hair behind her ear. 'That can wait.'

'Picture sandy, wet and tired kids needing baths

and dinner in two hours' time. Life will be much easier with a tidy kitchen.'

'Beautiful and practical.' He smiled down at her. 'Thanks.'

'Daddy!' The sound of Amber's running feet and the click-clack of Chester's claws on the wooden floor got louder.

'You're up, Dad,' she said, giving him a gentle push.

'See you soon.' He dropped an affectionate kiss onto her forehead before turning and catching Amber in his arms.

'Plane, Daddy.' Amber stretched out her arms.

Luke zoomed his squealing daughter up the hall and Chloe watched, smiling, as the two people she loved with all her heart shared so much fun.

She walked into the kitchen and stopped in surprise. Steph was pulling clear wrap over the remains of the moist chocolate beetroot cake Chloe had baked. 'I thought you were going to the beach?'

'I am. We are,' Steph said with a smile, 'but it's not fair to leave you with this mess. Two of us attacking it will halve the job and the time. Besides, with that lot out of the house, I can finally get some time to really thank you.'

Chloe ran some hot water into the sink, feeling embarrassed. 'You already did that when you arrived.'

Steph shook her head. 'Then I was thanking you for the nursing care. Now I'm thanking you for bringing my brother back into the world. He's a totally different man now, thank God.'

Chloe squirted detergent into the water. 'Most of that's because he no longer has a tumour in his brain.'

'I'm sure that's a part of it, but I haven't seen him this happy and content in a very long time.'

Using everything she had to stay strong, Chloe said, 'I'm glad, but I doubt it's me. I think it's helped that he no longer blames himself for Anna's death.'

'I can't help noticing how affectionate he is towards you,' Step said matter-of-factly.

'He's like that with everyone.' Chloe hoped the heat in her cheeks would be attributed to the steam rising from the sink.

'No, he's not.' Steph's questioning gaze zeroed in. 'Medically speaking, Luke's able to live alone now, isn't he?'

'Yes.' The moment the tiny yet loaded word escaped her lips Chloe wanted to suck it back.

'And your stuff's still in the bathroom.'

It's not a question. She's looked and seen. Stunned at the directness of the conversation, Chloe stared at Luke's sister, unable to form a coherent sentence.

'I know how ridiculously independent my brother can be, and if he didn't want you in his house, he'd have asked you to leave. I imagine if you didn't want to be here either, you would have left too.'

'Do you put all of Luke's friends in the witness box?'

Steph gave her shoulder a squeeze. 'Sorry. It's just I haven't seen him this at ease since before Anna died, and I know the reason is you.'

Chloe's hands jerked on the plastic bowl she was washing, sending suds spraying everywhere. The image of Luke always closing his eyes when he touched her burned her brain and she didn't want Steph to get the wrong idea. 'Luke doesn't love me, if that's what you're getting at.'

'I know my brother and I recognise when he's in love.'

Her heart did a ridiculous lurch and she turned to look at Steph. 'Really?'

She nodded. 'You love him too, don't you?'

There was no point denying it. 'I do but…'

'There don't have to be buts.'

She chewed her lip. 'There do,' she said, remembering Jason. 'I had a hysterectomy. I can't give him a child.'

Steph silently passed her a towel. 'This conversation suddenly needs wine.' She opened a bottle and poured two generous glasses. Taking a seat at the table, she said, 'Luke has a child. His need to be a father has already been fulfilled, so don't spend a moment worrying that will be a problem. Do you love Amber?'

'Of course I do,' Chloe said with surprising heat.

'Good.' Steph nodded, her face filling with empathy. 'I never had any problems having the kids and I can't imagine how it must feel knowing you can't have a child of your own. I wish I could help.'

Chloe found herself trying to make Steph feel less guilt about her own fertility. 'That's very kind of you but, short of surrogacy, there's nothing you or anyone can do.'

Steph stared at her as if she'd just been hit and winded.

'Are you okay?'

Steph nodded vaguely, as if she'd been distracted and had lost the thread of the conversation. 'I'm fine. So you've enjoyed spending time with Amber?'

Chloe sucked in her lips and blinked. 'I used to avoid children because it was all too painful. But Amber's such a joy in my life.'

'She's a sweetie, that's for sure. And she'd make the cutest flower girl at a wedding.' Steph winked.

Luke's still wearing a wedding ring. Chloe shook her head as reality dumped over her like cold water. 'You're jumping the gun, Steph. Luke and I haven't even discussed beyond next week, let alone the future.'

'Well, from what I've seen today and the way you two are playing house with Amber, the future's looking pretty damn rosy.' Steph raised her glass and grinned at her. 'I'm never wrong, you know. Talk to him.'

I know my brother and I recognise when he's in love.

The words gave her permission to let her mind wander back to the night in the shower. *I missed you.* The memory of his tender touch on her body sent a shiver through her and she started cataloguing all his little affectionate touches—the way he slung his arm over her shoulder, tucked her hair behind her ear, and moments like just a short while ago when he'd checked she was included in his family's trip to the beach.

All of it said he cared. Really cared. Was Steph right? Did Luke love her? Had she been so busy being fearful that, like her father and like Jason, he didn't love her that she'd purposely focused on all the wrong things in self-defence? Like a wedding ring that had been part of him for a decade so that he might not even notice he still wore it? Or that closing his eyes when he touched her and when they made love was really just to savour her taste and her feel?

Had concentrating on those things blinded her to the many and oh-so-very right signals?

You'll never know if you don't ask.

And therein lay the problem. The idea of asking him both excited and terrified her in equal measure.

'If I can survive my sister's family ripping through the cottage like a tornado, then going back to work will be a breeze,' Luke said, his voice filled with laughter. He sat down next to Chloe on the two-person swing chair out on the deck.

Chloe leaned into his open arms, loving the feel of snuggling in against his chest and the steady beat of his heart. The sounds of the waves lulled her, along with the gentle movement of the seat. She sighed, enjoying the peace now that the Markham family had left and Amber was fast asleep.

'Your nieces are totally full on but gorgeous. How can Marty and Steph look so relaxed after spending two months confined with those three powerhouses in a four-wheel drive and a tent?'

Luke laughed. 'Steph loves it. If she had things her way, she'd have another baby at the drop of a hat and...'

Chloe glanced up at him, wondering why he'd stopped talking, and she met green eyes filled with apprehension. 'What?'

'Sorry.' He pressed a kiss into her hair. 'I didn't mean to upset you by talking about people who can make choices about whether or not to have children.'

Tears burned in her eyes at yet another example of his solicitousness, and her heart swelled. Steph's words, *I know when my brother's in love,* which had been playing across her mind for the last five hours, gained even more volume.

She ran her fingers down his arm. 'It's kind of you to worry about me but, really, I'm fine. I didn't even get a twinge when I saw Kate in her maternity uniform.'

He smiled down at her. 'Good for you.'

'I think looking after Amber's really helped me get things into perspective about children.'

He wound some strands of her hair around his fingers. 'I'm glad. You're amazing with her.'

'She's easy to love.' And she was. Endearingly easy.

'Most kids are.' He kissed the top of her ear and followed it by tracing the edge with his tongue.

Her body liquefied at the erotic touch but her brain screamed, *This is it. Your opportunity to tell him how you feel.*

'Now you're close to going back to work, I guess I'm wondering where this is going.'

He blinked at her—his gaze slightly out of focus. 'Where what's going?'

'This. Us.' She stretched out her arm to encompass the deck and the cottage. 'Sharing the care of Amber, sharing a house.'

He stilled. 'Aren't you happy?'

She smiled, her heart so full it was overflowing. 'I'm deliciously happy.'

'So am I.'

He cupped her cheeks with his hands, gently caressing the skin with his thumbs, and then he kissed her—deep, long and hard.

Her body slackened, craving him and preparing for him.

Focus. Tell him first. Celebrate second.

Somehow she forced strength into her wobbly limbs and sat up, planting her feet firmly on the ground.

His eyes sparkled with anticipation. 'Inside? Good idea. Sex on this swing will land both of us on the deck.'

'I don't want to go in just yet. Luke...' Her mouth stalled at the words she needed to say.

He smiled expectantly at her, waiting for her to continue.

Just tell him. He's shown you a hundred different ways that he loves you. Heck, his sister even noticed. It's going to be fine.

'Luke, I've changed since we met.'

He picked up her hand. 'I know, you said. You're at peace with your infertility and that's great.'

She shook her head. 'I don't mean that. Well, I sort of mean that.'

Bemusement crossed his face. 'You're not making a lot of sense.'

'Sorry.' She met his gaze. 'I love you.'

He stared at her, surprise clear on his handsome face. 'No.' Incredulity clung to the tiny word.

She smiled at him, understanding his disbelief and urging him to believe her. 'I know I said I'd never allow myself to fall in love again but I was wrong. I've realised that up until I met you I was never in love. This thing between us is nothing like I've ever known. I love you and Amber with all my heart.'

He stood up so fast that the momentum sent the swing careening wildly. Crossing the deck, he reached the railing and gripped it tightly, his knuckles gleaming white in the moonlight. 'We're friends, Chloe, remember? No commitments, casual, easy, that was the deal.'

He hurled the words she'd spoken a few weeks ago right back at her, the tone both accusatory and horrified. Her heart stung with the slap of them.

Make him understand. 'I know that's what I said, what we agreed to, and I meant it at the time. I had no plans to ever love again, but it's happened.'

She thought about all the tiny, thoughtful things he'd done for her over the weeks, adding them together where they added up to one big thing— love. Walking over to him, she rested her hand on his shoulder. 'I don't think I'm the only person here who's changed.'

He shrugged her hand away and faced her. 'What are you talking about?'

'I think you love me too.'

Raw horror streaked across his face, dominating every other emotion. It reached out like the bony hand of the grim reaper and grasped her tightly around the throat, crushing her larynx. Crushing her soul. She anticipated what was coming next and she wanted to cover her ears so she didn't have to hear his words.

'I love my wife, Chloe. I've only ever loved Anna.'

The softly spoken words shattered her heart into a thousand damaged and jagged pieces. She bit into her fist to stop herself from crying out. What had possessed her to listen to his sister? Why had she gone against her better judgement and ignored what she knew to be true and instead dared to dream?

Foolish, stupid, idiotic Chloe.

His green eyes—racked with a tight tangle of indecipherable emotions—sought her gaze and she let him pull her into his arms.

'You're incredibly special to me.' He stroked her hair. 'I'm extremely fond of you, and Amber and I want you here with us. Nothing has to change.'

Feeling battered and bruised, her head fell against his shoulder as if she could no longer hold it up on her own. Resting there, in her favourite place, she breathed in his scent of salt, sand and musk and again felt the thud of his heart beating against her breasts—solid, rhythmic, life affirming.

Nothing has to change.

She could so easily continue living here with the two people she loved in just the same way as she had for the last few weeks. A picture of it formed in her mind.

Something deep inside her snapped.

A king wave of long-contained, life-damaged

emotions dating back to her childhood washed through her with a deafening roar, strewing and spewing debris until it filled her to overflowing.

Nooooooooooooo.

Everything has to change.

Value yourself.

Her very first memory was a look of disappointment on her father's face. No matter what she'd done or said, it had never been enough to earn her father's love, and then he'd shunned her in her darkest hour. Her love hadn't been enough for Jason and now it wasn't enough for Luke.

Luke's betrayal hurt the most. He was the *one* man she'd thought was different. The one man, with the exception of her brother, who had treated her with honour and respect. His many and varied considerate actions—like remembering exactly how she liked her coffee and noticing when she was feeling strung out and insisting she take a break—had combined with a heap of other tiny but thoughtful things to show her that he truly cared for her. Loved her.

How wrong she'd been.

She might have got that wrong but one thing

she did know was that she didn't deserve to be treated like this—like a second-class citizen begging for affection. She deserved so much more.

You've never asked for more from anyone.

It's time to start.

Her shattered heart started cobbling itself together—ragged and bleeding—readying itself to put on the fight of its life.

Luke patted Chloe consolingly on her back in a similar way he did with Amber when she was upset. His mind strained and creaked, feeling as dazed and as confused as it had just after his surgery. He had no idea where Chloe's unexpected declaration of love had come from, but he was desperately hoping it was an aberration and she'd let it go. She'd told him emphatically that she didn't commit, that she didn't want a relationship, which was the only reason he'd had sex with her.

The only reason?

He refused to answer his own question.

Chloe raised her head and stepped out of his embrace. 'You're *fond* of me?'

'Of course I am.' He smiled encouragingly. 'Like I said, you're incredibly special to me.'

If her eyes had been lasers, he'd have been burned to a crisp. 'You're fond of Mr Megat's satay, Luke. You're fond of Chester. I am neither one of those things.'

He trod carefully, knowing there were un-exploded mines everywhere. 'I never said you were.'

'No, you didn't,' she said flatly.

Her grim expression didn't offer him any hope that the fact he hadn't said the words was a good thing. He ran his hand over his head and sighed. 'I don't understand where all this is coming from. I thought we were happy with the way things are.'

'*You're* happy with the way things are.' Her voice rose, edged with steel, and it carried out into the night air. 'And why wouldn't you be? After all, I cook, I clean and I look after Amber. Hell, I'm the housekeeper you get to have sex with.'

A flame of rage licked at the edges of his control. He hated the way she'd just reduced what they'd shared into something mean and squalid. 'Hey, who's been doing the cooking and the cleaning and the bulk of the childcare recently while you've been at work?'

'You want a medal or a chest to pin it on?'

'Now you're being juvenile.'

She threw her arms out. 'Am I? I don't think so. The thing is, Luke, I don't exist to make your life easier. That is not my sole purpose in life.'

'I know that.' He hardly recognised the woman in front of him and he reached for her, wanting to convince her she was very wrong, but she dodged him.

'Never for one moment have I ever thought that. In fact, I've worked hard at making it clear to you how much I appreciate everything you do for us.'

A flicker of something close to sorrow flashed across her face. 'Yes, you've done that extremely well. I've felt very appreciated, which is part of the problem.'

'I don't understand.'

She gave him a pitying look. 'I'm a woman with feelings, Luke, and a huge capacity to love.'

Guilt clawed at him like the talons of a bird of prey. 'I've never hidden from you that I love Anna.'

Her chin shot up and he saw regret shining brightly in her eyes. 'You're right, you haven't. I just thought you loved me, too.'

Her pain barrelled into him. 'I'm sorry, Chloe. I never meant for you to get the wrong impression about us. Anna and I...' He fought to find the words to describe the love they'd shared. 'It only happens once.'

She closed her eyes and swayed.

He shot out his hand, closing his fingers around her upper arm to steady her, worried she was going to faint.

She opened her eyes and pulled away from his grasp so fast it was as if his touch had burned her.

'Chloe, please.'

She shook her head and wrapped her arms around herself. 'You've made things very clear, Luke. You don't love me so I have to go.'

Panic exploded. 'I'm not asking you to leave. Those two things aren't mutually exclusive, Chloe.'

Her eyes widened beyond what he'd thought possible. 'Yes, they are.'

'Yesterday they weren't.' He threw out his

hands in frustration at her behaviour. 'Chloe, you can't just change the rules without notice.'

'Goodbye, Luke.'

The thought of her leaving gutted him but rising fury took hold. She was being illogical and irrational. She'd just turned their agreement upside down by expecting more. She was the one being totally unreasonable. He lashed himself to his anger—the safest of all his roiling and chaotic emotions—and he fought back. 'So you're leaving, just like that? At ten o'clock at night? What about Amber? You said you loved her.'

Pain slashed her face. 'I do.'

'Well, you've got a funny way of showing it. She's not going to understand why you're suddenly not here any more. Why you've abandoned her. She lost her mother and now—'

'Don't you *dare* lay a guilt trip on me,' she said, her voice deathly quiet. 'I'll explain it to her.'

Incredulity poured through him at the thought. 'And exactly how are you going to do that?' he yelled, giving up all pretence at trying to be the calm and logical one. 'She's barely two.'

For a moment Chloe looked torn and defeated

but then she squared her shoulders. 'Chester and I will take her for walks on the beach so she can still spend time with us. I'll ease out gently.'

He didn't want to think about Chloe and Chester on the beach, playing with Amber, without him. Or about her easing out of his life. 'And if I don't allow you to do that?'

Shock and devastation filled her eyes. 'As her father you could do that but I hope you'll be adult enough to set aside how you feel about me and do what's in her best interests.'

He hated the way she was looking at him as if she loathed him. Damn it, this wasn't his fault. Did she think she could just turn their lives upside down with no warning and have everything her own way? 'You do realise this has to go both ways? You know Amber sleeps better at night when Chester sleeps at the end of her bed.'

Chloe bit her lip. 'I guess there can be access arrangements with Chester. He can sleep over occasionally.'

This is what getting divorced must be like.

The thought skidded across his mind before being buried by his resentment that she was ruining something that had worked so well for both of them. For Amber. For all of them.

She wants my love.

His heart threw off a crazy beat. Could he say it? Could he tell her that he loved her? 'So all of this angst could have been avoided if I said I loved you?'

Her eyes narrowed. 'And meant it.'

He thought of Anna—the love of his life since he'd been seventeen—and the words died on his lips. 'I can't lie to you, Chloe.'

A tremble whipped across her body. 'I know. I've always known.' She walked briskly to the French doors. 'Box up my stuff, text me a time when you're not here and I'll come over and collect it, and then I'll leave my key.'

The deck felt like it was tilting under his feet. 'There has to be another way, Chloe.'

'There isn't.'

She stepped inside, picked up her bag and her dog and without a backward glance walked out the front door into the night.

The ensuing silence suffocated him.

CHAPTER TWELVE

'I'M CHASING PEOPLE for extra hours, Chloe, and as you're our most flexible staff member I'm starting with you first,' Keri said, her expression hopeful.

'Sure.' *The more hours the merrier.*

No, scrub that. Nothing was merrier, but more hours at work meant less time to think about how her life had imploded so dramatically forty-eight hours ago. She was happy to stockpile hours and money because she had less than a month to find a new position. A new job far, far away from the plastics ward.

She'd been up all hours, tweaking her résumé, and had applied for a job in Paediatrics as well as one in the cardiac surgery unit. She really didn't want to leave Gold Coast City but just in case those two jobs didn't work out, she'd also applied to the only private hospital where Luke didn't have admitting rights.

The job of her heart was the paediatric job— her way of being with children—but in the short term she'd take anything on offer because there was no way she was working on the plastics ward when Luke returned from sick leave. She just hadn't told Keri that yet.

'Great,' Keri said, writing on the roster. 'I'll slot you in for Friday between five and seven p.m.'

Chloe frowned. 'Actually, Friday's the hospital barbecue.'

Keri nodded. 'And the family carnival, which is why I'm asking you.'

Because I don't have a family. Her heart, so badly battered and bruised, barely had the energy to react. 'Actually, I'm taking Chester...'

Keri laughed. 'It's designed for children, not dogs, Chloe. He'd run amok in the petting zoo and he won't be allowed to use the bouncy castle.'

'No, but Amber will.'

Interest flared in Keri's eyes. 'You're taking Amber?'

'I am.' It would be her first visit with the little girl since she'd left the cottage and she couldn't wait to see her. She bit her lip, not wanting to think about how she and Luke had organised the arrangements via text. Short, sharp, brief, impersonal texts from Luke with the subtext of bitter acrimony.

'But I spoke to Luke yesterday when I was running through the plastics department's RSVPs,' Keri said, her forehead creasing. 'He told me he isn't coming.'

'That's right.' *Because I am.* She bit her lip to stop the threat of tears that permanently threatened to spill and she picked up the fluid balance charts to shut out the bewildered look he'd worn on his face when she'd left him.

You caught him unawares. He'd believed you when you'd said you'd never love again.

She stomped on the temptation to feel guilty. She couldn't afford guilt if she was to stay standing.

'I guess he has another appointment.' Keri sounded disappointed.

'I guess so. I offered to take Amber because she likes bouncy castles.' She wanted the conversation over. 'I can fill in on the roster for any other days in the next two weeks. Email me the dates and times.'

It was bad enough that Luke couldn't love her. She wasn't adding to her pain by disclosing to anyone at the hospital how much of a fool she'd made of herself. No, she was keeping the whole sordid episode to herself.

It wasn't sordid. They were the best weeks of your life.

Right up to the moment he told you he couldn't ever love you.

The ache that had become part of her burned again.

She swallowed against it, reminding herself that the alternative to staying with Luke while knowing that he didn't love her would be worse than this.

How is that possible?

She didn't know the answer to that. All she knew was that she had to value herself, because if she didn't, no one else would. If Luke couldn't love her then they couldn't be together. She just had to get through these first dark days. She was a survivor and she'd keep doing what she needed to do by taking one step at a time. She'd get through one hour, one shift, one day and one entire night—one long, lonely and excruciatingly empty night at a time.

She'd already got through two. Just.

Thank goodness for her beloved dog. Only he too was sad, desperately missing Luke and Amber and whimpering at night while she silently cried. He'd stare at her with a puzzled look in his big, brown eyes and then lick her tears. She'd broken all the rules, and Chester now slept on her bed as she stared at the ceiling and told herself she'd done the right thing. Was doing the right thing.

Giving herself a shake, she made a decision. Tomorrow she'd ring Nick and Lucy and offer to mind the twins so they could have a date. The babies would keep her so busy she'd have no time to think about Luke, Amber and everything she'd lost.

It was worth a shot.

* * *

'Night-night, Amber,' said Luke, tucking his daughter in.

'Where Clo? Want Clo.'

Luke sighed. This conversation had become his nightly routine since Chloe had left. 'You'll see her tomorrow.'

'Chester?' Amber asked hopefully.

'And Chester.'

The house was so quiet without the antics of the puppy that Luke had actually gone online earlier and typed *'Child-friendly dog'* into a browser after he'd heard himself call Chester to come for a walk. Hell, he'd even asked Chloe for an opinion on an issue concerning the foundation before realising she was no longer in the cottage.

If he hadn't seen a recent MRI of his brain, he'd be convinced he was losing his mind.

He kissed Amber. 'Sleep tight, blossom.'

For the first time in two nights Amber snuggled down without further delays.

As he quietly closed her door, relief trickled through him that things might be finally getting back to normal.

What's normal? Things haven't been normal since Anna died.

But they'd been normal with Chloe.

He struggled with the thought. How could that be? He still missed Anna. Granted, it wasn't the same desperate loneliness it had been at the start when half of him felt like he'd died too, but he still felt her absence.

He walked into the laundry and smoothed out some clothes for Amber to wear tomorrow, justifying that within the hour they'd be crushed, so there was no point in ironing them. The truth was he didn't have the energy. All the domestic tasks he'd got such a sense of satisfaction from doing these last few weeks were suddenly chores.

That's because you did them with Chloe.

Now she'd gone and the house was dismal. Why the hell had she fallen in love with him and ruined something that was working so well? He'd been asking himself *that* question over and over since she'd left.

Because you told her you didn't love her.

He hated the answer and a fizz of anger stirred.

There's no crime in loving my wife.

He did a desultory toy tidy-round as much to shut out his unwanted thoughts as to avoid an injury to his feet. He picked up a board book and as he rose he came face to face with Anna's photo. He picked it up and her blue eyes stared out at him as if she knew everything about him.

She did.

They'd grown into adults together. Made two five-year plans together, dreamed of having four children and enjoying a long and happy future, only to experience a vastly shortened version of it. 'It should have been longer, Anna.'

She didn't reply. She never did, and now the memory of her voice in his head was muffled and barely discernible. In all their years of being a couple, they'd never had a conversation about one of them dying young, or what either of them thought the remaining partner should do in that event. Why would they? They'd expected a lifetime together, and he'd never pictured his life with anyone else.

He returned the photo to the side table where it sat next to a specimen vase containing a single strand of pink and white Singapore orchids.

Chloe.

It was a typical, caring, Chloe gesture. She was truly amazing and it wasn't that he didn't value her or care for her deeply—he did—but he couldn't switch love on and off and it was unfair of her to expect him to do that.

He dumped the toys into the basket and noticed the three spherical sand spinifex grass heads Amber had collected on the beach the day Steph had visited. He would have made Amber leave them at the back door but Chloe had brought them inside and placed them on the bookshelf. It was a simple decorating touch—connecting the indoors to the outdoors—and their golden colour contrasted perfectly with the dark, polished wood, adding warmth to the cottage.

He moved into the kitchen and was greeted by the newly framed and hung painting that Amber had made at daycare. She'd insisted the bright yellow splotch of paint was Chester and the blue blob was herself. Chloe had printed the date on the bottom right-hand corner and had written in her neat handwriting, *'Chester and Amber at the beach.'* He smiled at the bright, primary colours that dominated the otherwise empty wall, giving the kitchen heart.

A breath-sucking jolt thudded through him. This was the only painting in the house. When he'd moved in, he hadn't cared about decorating. He frantically glanced around him, suddenly seeing the cottage with new eyes. His coffee was in labelled containers and the tea towels matched. He backtracked into the main room. A vase of cheery daisies sat on the coffee table, and a bowl filled with assorted shells and coral surrounded a scented candle that he remembered Chloe lighting one night after Amber had gone to bed. Through the window, out on the deck, he could see the shadows of the hardy, salt-resistant yucca plants in their funky containers. Chloe had suggested he buy them from the farmers' market and use them to soften the utilitarian space.

Somewhere along the line, in the last few weeks, the cottage had gone from being a house to a home.

Chloe had changed it.

When he'd moved in, it had been just a place to live that didn't hold haunting memories of Anna.

He'd existed in it rather than lived in it. Chloe had made the cottage a space he felt comfortable in, somewhere he wanted to be—a place he belonged.

Not in the last forty-eight hours.

His gut lurched. He missed her so much.

I'm the housekeeper you get to have sex with.

No. Acid burned his stomach as his entire body rejected her statement. Chloe was so much more to him than that. The domestic help she'd given him anyone could have done. It was everything else about her he valued. She'd made him laugh, she'd challenged him, and at times she'd infuriated the hell out of him. She'd shared the highs and lows of raising Amber with him, which he'd treasured. And when she hadn't been around, he'd thought of her constantly.

That's love.

No, it isn't.

He thought about Anna. How they'd loved and laughed, bickered over trivial things and had cried together when Amber was born. How he'd looked forward to coming home at the end of each working day to share his day with her and hear about hers. How he'd loved being married and having a life partner and a friend.

Chloe's been that to you, too. You love her.

I can't love her. I love Anna.

You love them both.

His breath stalled. There it was. Starkly simple. He'd been blessed with two amazing women in his life and he loved them both.

He'd never thought he was capable of loving another woman, he'd never thought he'd want to love someone else, but it had happened. Chloe had quietly moved into his cottage and into his heart, and in her calm and happy way had brought him back to life.

The guilt that had been plaguing him about her now made sense. For weeks he'd felt like he was having an affair, cheating on Anna and their life together. Now he could finally see that it hadn't been anything like that.

The twinge he always got when he thought about Anna came, but it felt different. Once a throbbing pain, it was now a mellow and mild ache. His love for her would always be a part of him—she'd been his first love and the mother of his child. Death didn't change that.

Peace settled over him, and for the first time since the car accident he no longer wanted to fight the change that had been foisted on his and Amber's lives. He wanted to embrace it. He tugged off his wedding ring. Chloe was part of that change.

It only happens once.

Nausea rolled in his stomach. He'd told the woman he loved that he could never love her.

Urgency spun through him. He had to tell her he'd been stupid and wrong and he had to do it now. He grabbed his phone and punched in Steph's number.

His sister answered promptly. 'Hey, Luke, what's up?'

'I seriously need your help.'

'What's wrong? Is it Amber?' Panic threaded through her voice.

'No, she's fine.' He rubbed the stubble on his head. 'No one's physically hurt.'

'You're not reassuring me here,' she said,

sounding like she was sensing his desperation. 'You never ask for help.'

'It's Chloe. I love her.'

She laughed. 'That's not a secret, Luke.'

He rubbed his jaw. 'It was to me until five minutes ago.'

A short silence wavered on the line before a sigh broke it. 'Oh, Luke…'

The gravity of what he'd done to Chloe forced his eyes closed for a moment. 'Yeah. I need to talk to her. Can you come over and stay with Amber? Right now?'

'See you in fifteen.' The line went dead.

Chloe was flicking through a magazine. She'd tried reading a book but she couldn't concentrate, so she'd gone for something lighter. Celebrity gossip wasn't working either. She glanced at the clock. Nine p.m. She was on duty at seven in the morning so she should probably go to bed but really there was no point because sleep would elude her.

Chester suddenly sat up, his ears pricking up,

and then he shot out of his basket, raced to the door and barked at it.

He never barked at the door. 'Quiet, Chester,' Chloe said, dropping the magazine onto the couch. 'Back to your bed.'

Chester ignored her, his barking becoming louder and more frantic. Over the noise, Chloe heard knocking.

She peered through the peephole.

Luke.

She blinked and peered again, not believing the image her eye was seeing.

Luke paced back and forth outside her door.

Slipping her hand around her now frantic dog's collar, she opened the door. Chester lunged forward, all slobbering tongue and love-me-Luke Labrador adoration, desperate for a pat from the man who'd broken her heart.

You're a traitor, Chester.

'This is an unexpected visit,' she said, noticing that the dark shadows under his eyes, which had vanished in recent weeks, had returned.

Luke nodded. 'May I come in?'

No. Yes. 'Why?'

'I need to talk to you,' he said, keeping his gaze fixed on her face as he reached down and patted Chester. 'And neither of us wants your neighbours to hear our conversation.'

Her bleeding heart dripped some more. 'I don't want to hear our conversation. You made yourself perfectly clear the other night.'

He flinched. 'Chloe, please. May I come in?'

Oh, God, what if he wants to cancel my time with Amber? The thought terrified her, but as much as she didn't want him in her apartment, because it was her Luke-free zone, she also knew she wasn't prepared to risk losing access to Amber. Sighing, she turned away from the door. Leaving Chester with Luke, she walked back into her apartment and stood by the balcony doors.

Luke gave Chester a super-fast cuddle in the hope it would calm the dog down and then he dumped him in his basket and said, 'Stay.'

The puppy looked up at him, all woebegone and filled with disappointment, but thankfully he obeyed the sternness in Luke's voice.

Chloe, on the other hand, looked remote and detached. Everything about her lovely, lush body was sharp and angular, as if she was surrounded by protective steel pickets—pickets he'd put there.

'How are you?'

Great start, Luke. Nothing like inane social chitchat after you've broken someone's heart.

'Fine.'

Her face was drawn and exhaustion clung to her. 'You don't look fine.'

She pressed her hands against the back of the couch. 'Why are you here, Luke?'

'Can we sit down?'

She shook her head.

He rubbed the back of his neck as her animosity rolled into him. He'd planned his speech out in his head and it started with both of them sitting down and him holding her hand.

Not going to happen, pal.

'I love you, Chloe.'

She blinked at him and then she laughed—a bitter, twisted sound that plunged deep into his heart. 'This *is* very unexpected, given you told me you're a one-woman man.'

'I was. I am.' He implored her to understand.

'Oh, and that really clears things up.'

Her sarcasm whipped him. Hell, none of this was coming out how he'd rehearsed it.

'I've missed you, Chloe. The house is so empty without you.'

The shards of brown in her eyes sparked like flint. 'I think you're confusing missing me with missing my domestic and child-rearing help.'

'That's ridiculous and you know it.' But as his defensive tone hit the air, he acknowledged his culpability.

'Do I?' Her hands hit her hips. 'I feel used, Luke. Like I was convenient to you for a time right up until I asked for something, and then I was discarded.'

He shook his head and a wry smile tugged at his lips. 'You're a lot of things, Chloe, but convenient was never one of them.'

Her head jerked up. 'That's supposed to make me feel better?'

Discarding every idea he'd come up with on the drive over, he crossed the room and kneeled on the couch so he was facing her. 'From the moment I saw you that first day at the hospital when I was organising a nurse for Made, you've turned my life upside down. You've made me feel things I hadn't felt in months and months. You brought me out of my fog of grief and back into my life, but as amazing and wonderful as it was, as it is, it scared the hell out of me.'

Chloe stared down into his face, matching up his words with the heartfelt feelings on his face. He was speaking the truth. 'Why did it scare you?'

'Because it felt like I was cheating on Anna.'

'Oh.' She didn't know what else to say as she tried to absorb the unexpected information.

'You told me the other day that you felt very appreciated by me and that was part of the problem. I didn't understand what you meant then, but I do now. I realise I've been in love with you for weeks. You noticed it, Steph noticed it and probably the entire neighbourhood noticed it,' he said drily. 'I was too busy running from it to recognise it as love.'

She thought about how much she loved him and if that was even a tenth of how he'd felt about Anna, she now understood. 'Because you felt like you were betraying Anna by loving me.'

Relief flooded his face. 'Yes. That's it exactly, but I now see that's so very wrong. Crazy even.'

She didn't resent Anna Stanley, but she wouldn't be a normal woman if she didn't have some concerns about his love for herself, given what he'd just told her. 'You said that love could only happen once for you.'

'I was stupid.' He pressed his hand over hers. 'I now see and understand how untrue that statement is. I've loved Anna and I love you. I've been blessed to know the love of two good women.'

She bit her lip. 'I'm not Anna, Luke. I can't be her. I can only be me.'

He nodded frantically. 'I only ever want you to be you because that's who I've fallen in love with. I loved Anna and my love for her is in our memories and the legacy of her that lives in Amber.' He put his hand against her cheek. 'My love for you is a living, breathing thing.

'I know without a moment's doubt or hesitation that I love you. Truly love you. I love waking up in the morning with your fragrance on my pillow, I love how you sing off-key in the shower, how you dance around the house with Amber and how you've brought so such wonder and delight to my life.'

He really does love me for me.

Her heart fired happiness into every part of her. 'I love you, too.'

'Thank God.' He smiled up at her and still on his knees said, 'Please marry me and share my and Amber's lives?'

Joy flooded her. 'Yes.'

His arms wrapped around her and he lifted her up and over the back of the couch until she was sitting on his lap. He kissed her—a kiss of love and commitment and filled with desire.

She sighed and snuggled in against him, feeling like she was home. 'Luke, are you sure you're okay with not having more children?'

Green eyes hooked hers. 'I'm okay if you're okay.'

'Amber's a joy,' she said, thinking of her little girl.

He stroked her hair. 'She is, and I have everything I need with the two of you in my life, but this isn't all about me. Would you like her to have a brother or a sister?'

'An overseas adopted brother or sister?'

'Yes, or a biological one.'

A flicker of unease ran through her. 'You know that can't happen.'

He kissed her. 'Please hear me out.'

Putting his hands on her hips, he adjusted her slightly so she was looking directly at him. His eyes shone brightly with his love for her and she knew intrinsically he'd never hurt her despite the fact she knew she couldn't possibly have their child. 'I'm listening.'

'It could happen if we think outside the box. We could use IVF to have a child.'

Why was he saying this? 'Luke, I don't have a uterus to grow a baby in, and there's only been one or two uterine transplants that I know of and the recipients are yet to give birth.'

He rubbed her back. 'You don't have a uterus but Steph does. She's spoken to me and offered to be a surrogate.'

Short of being a surrogate... She gasped, remembering the conversation she and Steph had shared in Luke's kitchen. 'Your sister would do that for us?'

'Yes, if we wanted to try for a child of our own, she would.'

The rush of emotion hit her so hard she burst into tears.

'Hey, hey, it's okay,' Luke said, kissing her tears. 'We don't have to try if you don't want to. I'll support you in any decision you make. It's all going to be fine, no matter what.'

For years Nick had been her only family and suddenly she had a partner, a daughter, a sister and the possibility of another child. 'I'm…not…upset…' she sobbed out, as even more tears flowed. 'I'm…happy.'

Luke looked utterly bewildered. 'Really?'

'Really.' She sucked in a noisy breath and nodded. 'It's just a lot to take in.'

'Take your time. There's no rush to make any decisions.' He kissed her on the nose. 'Actually, there is one rush thing.'

'What's that?'

'Getting you and Chester packed up and back to the cottage with Amber and me, where you both belong.'

She smiled at him, every part of her tingling with happiness. 'Home.'

'That's right. Our home.'

She wrapped her arms around him and kissed him, pledging her love and her hopes for their future and receiving his in return.

Callie swallowed a sigh and squared her shoulders. The Gold Coast City Hospital's annual staff picnic was in full swing and blessed by perfect Queensland sunshine. The golden sand of the beach was warm and some families were enthusiastically entering the sand-sculpture competition, buoyed by the prize of a trip to Port Douglas. The sea rolled in light but perfect waves for those taking advantage of the learn-to-surf lessons, and the lifeguards watched carefully as people played in the shallows and further out in the sea kayaks.

Up on the grassed area above the sand line— under the towering Norfolk pines—the barbeque and kids' carnival was in full swing. With the aroma of onions and sausages on the air, little children squealed on the bouncy castle while adults and teens alike screamed on the rotor as the floor dropped away from their feet.

'Chloe, hi!' Callie called out rather too loudly, waving to catch the nurse's attention. She was frantically looking for some fellow single colleagues to do an activity with. So far, the only people she'd met were busy with their children.

Chloe returned the wave and made her way over. 'Hey, Callie. Isn't this great?' She positively bubbled with happiness.

'I guess. To tell you the truth, I always find it a bit daunting with so many couples and families en masse. Us single girls have to stick together, right?' She heard the tightness in her laugh and tried to smooth it out. 'Do you want to try a surfing lesson with me?'

Chloe smiled apologetically. 'Sorry, Callie, I—'

'Clo, look me.'

Both of them turned to see Luke striding towards them with his daughter high on his shoulders. She was waving at Chloe with one hand and holding out her other arm, which had a pink helium balloon tied to it.

When Luke drew level with them, he leaned

in and kissed Chloe firmly on the lips. When he broke away, he grinned and said, 'Hey, Callie. Have you heard? Chloe's agreed to marry me.'

The news broke over Callie with a combination of delight and dismay. The world was full of couples, and today they surrounded her. 'That's great news,' she said brightly. 'Congratulations to both of you.'

'Thanks.'

Chloe and Luke grinned goofily at each other until Amber lurched sideways, reaching for Chloe.

'I guess with the rug-rat you're not up for a surfing lesson.'

'Sorry,' Chloe said, not looking the least bit sorry at all as she swung Amber into her arms. 'We're off to the petting zoo, but after that Amber's going to her aunt's so perhaps we can catch up with you in the bar tent?'

'Sounds like a plan,' Callie said, knowing that from her point of view it wasn't a plan at all. New love and the all-encompassing happiness that went with it was particularly hard for her to cope with because it reminded her of how wonderful she'd felt when she'd married Joe and, by contrast, how it had all ended so bitterly.

Chloe's mention of the bar tent drove the idea of surfing lessons out of her head. Suddenly she could do with a drink.

She struck a course in the direction of the refreshment tent and a couple of minutes later she walked into the large marquee. Half of it was open to the air and the other half was enclosed. As she entered the roofed section, it took her eyes a moment to adjust to the gloom after being out in the bright light.

'Callie.'

She instantly recognised that slow and sexy American drawl, which seemed to give her name a third syllable. Cade was sitting at the bar.

He raised his glass to her. 'Let me buy you a drink.' She hadn't seen him since he'd helped her with her diagnosis of the abandoned baby—the day they'd worked together so easily and companionably. Part of her wanted some more of that simple, easy camaraderie. 'That would be *shout* you a drink,' she said with a smile as she slid onto the bar stool next to his. 'We'll get you talking like an Aussie yet.'

He grinned. 'You wanna beer?'

She shook her head. 'I'm more of a champagne girl.'

'That doesn't sound very much like an Aussie sheila,' he said, using the old-fashioned slang word for woman.

She laughed. 'Have you been taking language advice from an eighty-year-old?'

He tilted his head. 'So you're not a sheila?'

'I may have been if I'd been born in 1933.'

'I think the barman's been yanking my chain.' He tapped his glass on the bar. 'Stuart, a glass of champagne for Callie and I'll have another beer.'

'No worries, Doc.' The barman immediately dispensed the drinks.

She noticed Cade's dark brown hair was damp. 'Been swimming?'

'I tried the sea kayaking. What about you?'

'I...' She toyed with lying that she'd built a sandcastle.

'What?' His eyes dared her to speak.

Oh, what the hell. She didn't care what he

thought of her. 'I pretty much came straight to the bar.'

He laughed. 'Been that good a day, has it?'

'Actually, it was a great work day. I discharged home three babies. It's the bouncy castle chaos out there that I don't cope with so well.'

'So being here at the bar is more about being in an adults-only zone than the need for alcohol.'

She smiled at him, welcoming his understanding. 'Pretty much.'

'Yeah.' He took a slug of his beer. 'Working with sick babies is totally different from the mayhem out there. Kids kept running into my ankles.'

She raised her glass to him. 'To the kid-free zone.'

He clicked her glass and winked at her. 'To the adults-only zone.'

A shiver of lust rocked through her and she crossed her legs, trying to stop the tingling that burned at the apex of her thighs.

His gaze rolled over her body, admiration in his eyes.

She soaked it up, loving the way it made her feel like a vibrant, sexy woman.

'So, Callie, what are your plans for the evening?'

'I don't make plans, Cade. I just let things roll out and see where they take me.'

His eyes danced. 'I like the sound of that. Do you care for company?'

She gave him a wide smile.

EPILOGUE

'YOU'RE BREAKING MY hand,' Luke said quietly.

'Sorry,' Chloe said.

She crushed it even harder when she heard Nick say to Steph, 'One or two more pushes and our niece or nephew will be born.'

The labour ward was full to overflowing with her family and she could hardly believe that her baby—her and Luke's baby—was about to be born.

'That's good to hear,' Marty said with feeling, rubbing his hand. 'I'm not sure my fingers can take much more of this.'

'You and me both,' Luke said with a grin.

'Both wimps,' Steph muttered.

Marty wiped her brow. 'Quite right, sweetheart. You're the amazing one here.'

And she was. Chloe was in awe and filled with gratitude at the gift Steph was giving them. Together she and Steph had endured hormone injections and ultrasounds. Chloe had experienced the egg harvests and Steph the implantations. It had taken four attempts before they'd finally succeeded in creating a pregnancy.

Throughout it all Steph had been amazing. She'd taken to being a surrogate with the same gusto with which she approached life, and each day she'd shared the pregnancy with Chloe. When the baby had kicked for the first time, she'd called Chloe at two-thirty-nine a.m. to tell her. Chloe had attended every prenatal appointment and Steph had always told the staff, 'I'm just the incubator. Chloe's the mummy and I'm the doting auntie.'

Steph had shared everything, and Chloe couldn't have felt more involved or more grateful. Now this precious nine months was about to end. And everything was about to start.

Steph grunted and then the contraction hit. She leaned forward, gripping her knees, and pushed.

Chloe edged closer, peering over Nick's shoulder.

'You're doing great, Steph. Keep it going.'

'Arrggh.'

A flash of black, a gush of fluid and Nick said, 'The head's born and no cord around the neck.'

Chloe held her breath and glanced up silently at Luke.

He squeezed her hand.

The baby rotated, its face pink and squished, and then Steph pushed again. The shoulders slithered out and the body followed with the thick, pulsating cord across its legs.

Our baby. Her heart stuttered as she willed it to be healthy.

'Is it a niece or a nephew?' Steph asked, falling back onto a bank of pillows.

Nick grinned. 'Come on, Chloe and Luke. Come and learn the secret I've been keeping for twenty weeks.'

Luke nudged Chloe forward. 'You do it.'

She glanced at the baby's legs and her throat threatened to close as love poured through her. 'A little boy. Amber's got a brother.'

'Luke, cut the cord.' Nick held out the scissors.

Luke, his eyes shining bright with tears, accepted the scissors and severed the cord between the two clamps.

The baby gazed up at them both with huge, dark eyes as if he'd been here before and was re-making an acquaintance.

With trembling hands, Chloe wrapped their son in a bunny rug and picked him up, hardly able to believe this was their baby. Their own flesh and blood, given life by his aunt. 'Oh, Steph, I can't begin to thank you.' She kissed her sister-in-law as tears poured down her cheeks. 'He's beautiful.'

Steph grinned, despite her exhaustion. 'Of course he is. He's yours and Luke's child, not to mention my nephew.'

Luke put his arm around his beautiful wife's waist and gazed down at her and his son. 'He's got the Kefes's Greek nose.'

Chloe laughed. 'Poor little guy.' She placed her finger across the baby's palm and his fingers automatically gripped it. 'He's got your long fingers.'

'We should take him to meet Amber.'

His words tumbled out over Chloe's, matching them exactly.

'You go and do that while I get cleaned up,' Steph instructed. 'The girls will all be champing at the bit to meet... What are you going to name him?'

Luke met Chloe's eyes, confirming the name they'd discussed. She nodded, smiling at him. He looked at Steph. 'He's Steven, after you.'

'Oh.' His usually practical sister blinked rapidly. 'You didn't have to do that.'

He kissed her forehead. 'We wanted to. We can't thank you enough.'

She nodded. 'It's what family does. Now, go be the parents and do all the hard work.' She picked up her husband's hand. 'Marty and I are looking forward to being his aunt and uncle, spoiling him rotten and then handing him back for you to sort out.'

Luke kissed his sister and then ushered Chloe out of the ward to a waiting room where Nick's wife, Lucy, was minding all the children, along with her twins.

Amber, now four, jumped up the moment they walked into the room and raced up to them. 'Is it a girl?'

Chloe sat down on the couch and Luke picked up Amber, hugging her hard. 'You have a baby brother.'

Amber wrinkled her nose. 'Can I still cuddle him?'

'Of course you can,' Chloe said.

Luke sat down next to Chloe and popped Amber between them. Chloe carefully placed Steven in his sister's arms, supporting the baby's head. Luke supported his body.

'What do you think, Amber?'

'He's heavier than my doll.'

Chloe laughed and rested her head on Luke's shoulder. 'I can't believe this has really happened. That we could be this blessed.'

Luke stroked his son's head and ruffled his daughter's curls, knowing exactly what Chloe meant. Four years ago he'd never imagined he could ever be this happy again.

'I love you so much, Chloe Stanley.'

'I know you do, and I love you right back.'

She smiled at him in her serene way and he knew that everything was right in his world.

* * * * *